GIFTED

SAVANNAH KADE

GRIFFYN INK

Published by Griffyn Ink

www.griffynink.com

For ordering information or special discounts for bulk purchases, please contact Griffyn Ink at Mail@GriffynInk.com.

*D*on't do anything to your hair that you can't afford to keep up. If someone is discussing your roots it had better be about your great-great grandmother.

CHRISTIAN WEAVER WALKED THROUGH THE DOUBLE FRONT doors of Brighton Elementary School with more trepidation than a grown man should have.

Though he'd attended Brighton as a kid, this was not the same school. In the intervening years, the school had been moved, redesigned, and rebuilt. The only thing that remained the same was the name.

Instead of the sprawling one-story schoolhouse of his childhood, it was now a three-story cube with a lobby showing off trophies in a glass case. Signs with arrows indicated the direction to the principal's office and though he didn't want to go—*who did?*—Christian took a breath and headed that way.

The empty halls had his thoughts reverberating through his head. *Why had he let himself get roped into this?* He couldn't remember what specifically he'd done. Maybe he hadn't been happy enough at Sunday dinners, and this was his mother's solution. Maybe he didn't seem busy enough, or his mother thought there weren't enough elementary aged kids in his life. Whatever his mother's reason, it was too late for him now; he was already at Brighton.

Christian liked statistics. He liked numbers. He liked code. He was not overly fond of children. Volunteering in an elementary classroom was not on his bucket list. In fact, it might even show up in his definition of hell.

After trading his ID for a visitor badge, the woman at the desk told him to clip it to his shirt. She said this as though he was doing it wrong by holding it. Showing her as he clipped it on, he thanked her and headed out to find room 32.

While he climbed the stairs, he consoled himself with some numbers. He was a relatively tall man and a swimmer. Therefore, he probably outweighed at least three children together. Possibly four of them if they were small. If things turned, he believed he had a chance to fend off a few of them.

He'd also had karate classes as a kid and he could probably win in a fight, though, that wasn't the kind of thinking that was likely welcome in an elementary. His arms had to be longer than theirs, and he had to be taller, too, so he could probably put a hand on a small head to hold a wily child at bay.

But his next number failed him. *Two*. He only had two arms and there were certainly more than two children in the class-room. In his vivid imagination, he saw himself getting pulled under as a rogue flock of kids attacked him like piranhas. He hoped this teacher, Riley Zayat, would do a good job of keeping her students in line.

Maybe he didn't dislike children so much as he just didn't know what to do with them. He certainly didn't know what to do with children in groups and he wondered again why he'd let his mother talk him into this. In fact, why had she even thought this was a good match? He didn't know.

Sooner than he would have liked, Christian was standing in front of the door to classroom number 32. A bold sign on the door—clearly colored by children using a rainbow of crayons—said "Miss Zayat's Room."

Underneath that, the next line said only, *GIFTED*.

Taking a deep breath and wondering what fresh hell awaited him, Christian Weaver pushed open the door.

2

R iley looked up at the man who had—without knocking first—opened the door to her classroom. He stood frozen, not yet crossing the threshold.

"You must be Christian Weaver," she offered in her best teacher voice, but she only said it to be polite. There was very little doubt that this man was the son of Westerley and Dawson Weaver.

He had the older man's square jaw and his mother's bright green eyes. His brown hair, which came from both sides of the family, was surprisingly sun-bleached on the ends. Despite his height and the width of his shoulders, he stood in the doorway, looking at her warily as though she were some strange creature that might attack him.

"Come on in." She tried her best smile as she waved her hand, wondering if maybe he was a vampire and required an invitation.

Still, he didn't speak, but he stepped a cautious foot into her classroom. He looked around for a moment, taking in the smart-board at the front of the room, the clusters of small desks, and cluttered shelving that housed various projects. Riley got the impression he was absorbing all of it.

When he did finally speak, he said, "I thought there would be children."

That, at least, made her laugh. "There will be," she told him, "next time. Usually for the first meeting it's just me and the classroom. I try not to throw anyone to the sharks."

The panic on his face made her think that maybe he was taking her a little too seriously about the sharks. Then he took an obvious breath and asked, "If I'm volunteering to help with children. Why are there no children?"

"Well," she replied, "I thought you'd like to get to know the job first. I thought we'd go over what the class is doing and how you might best fit into that before we actually bring the children in. It's better to look like we know what we're doing."

He nodded at that and a small smile formed upon his lips.

Finally.

Her whole world was these kids. Her kids were complex, always needing more from her and asking questions she didn't have the answer to. It was why she used volunteer help whenever she could. The problem was that gifted kids needed gifted volunteers, and few gifted people were sitting around wondering what to do with their days. Westerley Weaver had been a godsend. She'd been volunteering for several years and recently brought in her niece, Bailey Ann Mayfair, to help with the smaller kids. Now, she'd said her own son would be a good match. But Riley was beginning to think Westerley's winning streak might be over.

Coming around from behind her desk, she stopped in front of him. She'd not done a full, proper introduction the way it was done here in the South. Holding her hand out, she said, "I'm Riley Zayat. The gifted teacher here at Brighton."

She watched as he cautiously shook her hand, his large fingers enveloping hers. Then he dropped the touch and stepped back, as if waiting. She guessed that made sense. If you weren't a teacher, you might not know what to do in a classroom, certainly not one like hers.

He towered over everything in the room. It was designed for kids, everything within reach for small people. Aside from her desk, it was all tiny. Christian Weaver was not going to fit. He became one more person for her to help fit in.

Realizing she needed to take the reins of the conversation, she turned and said, "I don't know what your mother told you but I have students ranging from second grade—the earliest age they can test into the gifted program here—all the way up through sixth."

Christian nodded at her but didn't say anything.

So Riley pushed on, "We work on special projects. I have each grade for three hours one afternoon a week. For example, I have second grade on Mondays, third graders on Tuesdays, and so on through the week. These kids are opted out of their regular classes to come to me, and it's my job to give them advanced and challenging curriculum."

He nodded again, but still seemed to have a little frown on his face. Riley recognized it. This was what she did—read mixed signals. She had to understand that when a child said their tummy hurt, it meant they had anxiety. That when they were suddenly lashing out at their friends, they were actually sick or scared or maybe something had gone wrong at home. And she had to understand that bright kids got easily bored and that many didn't understand how they fit in because they didn't.

Maybe he was one of them.

Given the way his mother talked about him, Riley thought that was entirely possible. She paused before speaking again. According to Westerley Weaver, Christian had sold his first computer program before he graduated middle school. She'd chattered as she reorganized one of the shelves. "He left high school a full year early, simply because he'd completed all the necessary coursework and didn't have any reason to stay." Though Westerley hadn't said it, Riley got the impression Christian hadn't been a social butterfly. He probably hadn't seen the value of walking at graduation. "I made him do the graduation ceremony and he didn't know anyone. It was the grade ahead of him. It was likely a mistake." She'd sighed. "He looked miserable the whole time and the pictures are terrible."

Riley had fought the laugh that bubbled up.

"He went to Cal Poly on scholarship and quickly graduated with honors in three years and—" Riley heard the buildup to Westerley's brag, but she'd not been prepared. "With three million dollars in his bank account! He won some contest for hacking something and got a big prize. He also made an app, but I still don't really understand it. He's been in Silicon Valley since then."

Three months ago, Christian Weaver had come home to Breathless, Georgia. The only explanation he'd given his mother was that he was bored. He'd bought a house. He showed up for Sunday dinners. He spent most of his days at his computer. His mother had no idea what he was doing, so she'd volunteered him in the same classroom where she worked.

Riley knew she was only getting half the story. It was possible none of the numbers were correct. But what Riley did know—because she'd researched him online and had the school do a background check—was that he *had* worked in Silicon Valley, and that he *had* bought a house for cash. And he *had* come back to Breathless approximately three months ago.

Now, she waved her hands around the classroom as she gave the short tour. Then, turning back to him, she said, "I suspect you'll fit best with my upper grades."

He spoke again, and something about it made her think he doled out his words carefully. "I'm assuming by *upper* you mean fourth, fifth, and sixth."

"Yes." She understood it wasn't *upper level* by most people's standards but for elementary school teachers it was. "I'm looking to have them do some robotics and maybe programming? You can see over here on the shelf we have a number of donated old pieces—" she didn't call it junk. "Alarm clocks, old dial telephones, things like that."

She watched as he carefully scanned the shelf, pointing to some of the loose wires, internal boards, dial pads not connected to anything. "It looks like somebody's already been taking them apart and trying to rewire things."

"And that's exactly my problem," Riley replied. "That's why your mother suggested you volunteer. I don't know anything about this, and I have three separate students in three different grades who've already been trying to create gadgets and I'm hoping you can help."

"What kind of *gadgets*?"

Apparently, he didn't really like that term. She noted it and moved on. "Well, one of the kids wanted to make a doorbell with the number pad. Another thought he could make a laser gun—"

She paused when Christian interrupted her with a bold laugh. For the first time, Riley looked at him like a grown man and not just a volunteer in her classroom. He had a stunning smile despite his standoffish manner.

Hopefully, he would do okay with the children. He had to. She didn't have an option. These were kids who were often too bright to fit in with their peers. Gifted class could make them even more ostracized. She was the one who gave them a place to belong. For some of these kids, she was fairly certain she was the only one.

Christian spoke through the grin that stayed on his face. "I can help one of your students make a laser gun. However, I really don't advise putting lasers in the hands of small children."

This time it was Riley who laughed. "I completely agree. I was thinking maybe something more like a laser pointer or a flashlight—a toy version."

"Okay," he nodded as he spoke, clearly thinking. "Do you want me to build it now?"

"I actually don't want you to build it at all. Just help the kids do however much they can. We have a project coming up. It's one of the last things we do before Christmas break. Each student picks a topic and we work together to create whatever it is. In some cases, they learn about an animal they're interested in. Some kids build a diorama. Some do a presentation on history and a couple of the children have said they would like to build a gadget of some sort." *Shit.* She'd said *gadget* again.

He nodded, but the frown looked like he still didn't understand.

She opted for more specific information as he'd latched onto that before. "I'm hoping that you can come in once, maybe twice a week. Help the kids with their projects. I can manage the project once we know what each child is working on, but I don't know what's feasible or when to stop them so they don't electrocute themselves." She paused. "Without you, we can't do any robotics or programming assignments."

He nodded then, and she was grateful. But the frown on his face made her wonder if maybe he was going to refuse.

She pushed. "Can you come back next week?" When he didn't say no, she pushed a little more and even added a day. "I'm hoping you can come for an hour each day Wednesday, Thursday, and Friday. The children are starting to pick their projects. I'd love if you'd help steer them. After that, we'll pick individual days that hopefully you can come in and help them build what they've chosen."

She knew her tone sounded hopeful, but she wasn't able to keep her voice clear of it. She had an advanced degree in teaching and was considered gifted herself. She wanted to be the teacher she'd needed. But even so, she had no idea how to help a kid wire a motherboard.

She needed Christian Weaver.

She held her breath waiting for him to say yes.

3

Riley took a deep breath and sat down at her desk. She looked around to make sure everything was in order for her students and for Christian to show up. She'd fucked up yesterday.

She'd told Christian to come at two, but that had been a mistake.

He'd walked into a classroom already full of fourth graders who jumped up, excited beyond measure, when the "robotics guy" came in. She guessed the kids were bored with her, but Christian was fresh meat. She also told them ahead of time that Christian knew about programming and lasers and more.

When he'd open the door, he'd been swarmed. It was clear by the look on his face that he was startled and unprepared.

"Are you Mrs. Weaver's son?" One kid had tugged Christian's sleeve and asked.

"Yes." But the word was so stilted Riley was afraid for him.

"She was my teacher volunteer last year," he said, and Christian nodded, not knowing what to do with the information.

Jacee knocked on his leg as though he was a door. "She wasn't my volunteer. I wasn't in this class until this year."

"Were you not gifted last year?" He'd frowned down at the child.

But Jacee just shrugged and said, "I guess I got gifted over the summer!"

Riley had been forced to call the kids off like an unruly pack of dogs. Given his comments from last week, she figured that was exactly what he'd been concerned about. She'd made the children *sit* and *stay* while she carved out some space for her erstwhile volunteer.

Crap. It wasn't a teaching moment she was very proud of. She apologized, of course, and she prayed he'd come back for the second day. He'd said he would, but Riley got the feeling it was only because he'd already promised to do so and not because he was looking forward to it.

That was her fault. Today, she was going to have him come in before the kids got here. Luckily, these were the fifth graders. They were a little bit older, noticeably more mature, and they would come in one or two at a time. Hopefully, it would be a little easier for Christian to take.

Last week she'd wondered how he'd interact with the kids. It was clear that he was incredibly smart and seemed he'd been a gifted kid himself. Though she knew the history of this school system, the gifted program hadn't been put into place until after he would have graduated. Her goal had always been to become the kind of teacher a kid like him would have needed.

In her hopes, Christian would recognize himself in the children and they would get on like a house on fire. Given the initial pack greeting, he'd been a bit stiff and formal all afternoon. She'd given him a chair and assigned the kids seats on the carpet, making sure he had a safe distance around him as he seemed to think the kids might launch forward and attack him at any moment.

On the other hand, he was incredibly good at answering their questions. His answers were relatively literal, but kids accepted a lot. Christian wasn't even "odd" so much as clearly uncomfortable. However, she had two kids in the fourth grade group who were on the autism spectrum. Both had taken to Christian and his straightforward answers.

"Can you program a robot to run like a dog?" Though Molly raised her hand, she asked her question before she'd been called on. Christian let it slide and Riley was grateful. Molly wasn't so much rude as she was oblivious.

"Yes," he'd looked directly at the little girl and answered with a smile.

Molly grinned and excitedly asked her follow-up, not seeing anything weird in his failure to elaborate. "Can you teach me to program a dog robot to run?"

"Probably," he replied, and Riley almost laughed at his blatant honesty.

But Molly had loved the answer, lighting up like a bulb. Despite the rocky start, Riley had counted it as a good day for the kids. She just needed to make it a good day for her volunteer, too.

There were seven kids from the third grade who had tested into the gifted levels. And Molly had a diagnosis of Autism Spectrum Disorder. Another kid had ADHD—the serious kind, not the kind where his parents just wanted to medicate him. Riley had encouraged his parents to test him, but they'd refused. She was doing her best, trying to get each child what they needed the most.

At the end of the first day, she'd sat down with Christian after the kids went back to their regular classrooms. Riley reviewed the kids' wishes with Christian. "Patrick is a bit of a history buff and already knows what he wants his project to be. Marcus is going to grow plants in different soils. Jenny wants to test various germs in petri dishes..." Riley tried to go fast by the ones that wouldn't affect Christian. "These two are up in the air. But Molly wants to build a robot dog that will run. *Shocking*."

Christian smiled back at her sarcasm, which she took as a

hopeful sign. He would have to do most of that work on that one. But he assured her it wasn't too big a project.

A fifth-grade child was hoping the "computer guy" could help make a doorbell for the classroom. That was the kind of thing Riley had thought was within the spectrum of her course. She warned Christian that was a possibility, and he'd agreed to that project as well. But then he'd looked at his watch and said he had to leave.

Riley hoped to finish the conversation today. She hadn't yet gotten around to explaining to him that all the projects had to be done by Christmas. Also, it was a good excuse to have him come early today... and *not* get swamped by kids.

When the door opened and he entered, she saw him wearing another pair of nice slacks and a long-sleeved thermal t-shirt. Though she hadn't noticed the first day, she had noticed yesterday. His t-shirt was very soft and the pants looked comfortable in addition to nice. As today was the third day she'd seen him, Riley decided she now had enough data to know that Christian Weaver had one outfit.

He certainly had it in several different colors, but he had one outfit. Luckily, the man was built. Though the thermal tees didn't show him off the way some guys liked, it was clear the man wasn't a slack.

"Here." She smiled at him and gestured across her desk as he came in. "I got you an adult size chair today. I'm sorry it took so long."

Smiling, he took the seat, for once not looking like he was getting tossed to a pack of dingoes. She'd called it. She also figured he'd appreciate getting down to business, as he seemed to want her to start the conversations. Not one to balk at having a volunteer with such special skills, Riley was more than willing to be accommodating.

"I don't want you to get overloaded. There are ten kids in today's class and twelve from sixth grade. You don't think building a robot and programming it to run like a dog is too much to accomplish between now and Christmas?"

"Well," Christian said, looking off toward the smart board. "I thought she said she wanted to make a robot dog run. I don't think there's enough time to build the whole robot. But there's certainly enough time to reprogram an already constructed piece."

Riley nodded. That made sense, but... "I don't have a quadruped robot and I don't know that her family does. I don't know *anyone* who does." This was often a problem with her class, just finding the right things for the kids to work with.

"Yes, you do," Christian said, not seeming to realize that robots didn't materialize out of thin air. "I have one."

Score one for Christian Weaver, she thought, but what she asked was, "Are you willing to share it with a *third grader*?"

He laughed. Then he smiled, revealing even white teeth and a twinkle to his eye that she didn't see much. But she liked it. Maybe his mother hadn't signed him up for torture, after all. Maybe he'd actually volunteered and the first days were just a little rocky.

"I'm willing." He crossed one leg over the other and leaned an elbow on her desk. She took that as a sign of comfort. "It's old. I built it years ago. So I know we can program it to run."

With a sigh, because she didn't want him to regret it later, Riley felt the urge to warn him. He seemed like a man who hadn't been exposed to elementary kids much. "What if it gets broken?"

"Then I'll fix it."

That was it. She wasn't going to push any further. He seemed to have no concerns about his robot, and Molly was already half in love with him. Riley wasn't going to making trouble where it didn't already exist.

Changing the subject, she told him, "Today's kids are slightly older," and she mentioned a few that she thought he might like to work with—ones who had shown an interest in his field before.

"Seven is the one who took apart the alarm clock and tried to hybridize it with the old dial pad phone." She smiled thinking about Seven. He'd came from a rough history, but he was sharp as a tack and willing to get into anything. "I had to explain to him that he couldn't unplug the things on my desk, strip the wires, and build my school equipment into something else."

Christian smiled. Maybe that was something he related to.

"I don't know what kind of project Seven will want to do, but I suspect you'll end up working with him."

She gave him two more names but by the end of the day Seven was the one who had picked a project that fully was in Christian's wheelhouse. Two others had chosen tasks that were going to need only a little help from her new volunteer.

Riley sent him home with a smile and breathed a sigh of relief. Good help was hard to find. Gifted kids needed adults who understood where they were coming from. Ones who handled odd turns in conversation and understood when they were bored and not just causing trouble. She did not want to overwhelm her new helper on the first week. But, if tomorrow came out okay, they could do this.

Besides, Riley was looking forward to having him back the next day.

❦ 4 ❧

*P*art of an opening conversation is often, "Who are your people?"
Your people had best be from the South.

"YOUR SISTER IS COMING TONIGHT. AND SO IS JACKSON. HE'S bringing his girls."

Christian nodded at his cell phone. He knew his mother couldn't hear him but it made him feel as though he were participating in the conversation. His mother often didn't leave him any room to do so. Today was no exception.

Christian would have asked if Aunt GiGi and Uncle Dex were also going to be coming but all he had to do was wait.

"GiGi and Dex are out of town this week. And that's why we have Jackson coming here with us."

Yup, Christian thought, then nodded at the phone again and waited. Most times he didn't even have to talk when they had a conversation.

"You're bringing your deviled eggs, right? You make the best deviled eggs." His mother said the same thing every time he agreed to come to Sunday dinner.

In this case, it was true. He did make the best deviled eggs.

He'd hated deviled eggs as a kid, but that was because relish drove him bonkers. But then his Aunt GiGi made him a batch without pickle relish and he'd eaten the whole plate. He'd been about six at the time.

So Christian had become a deviled egg chemist. He knew his mother still preferred her eggs with relish, but she allowed him to make the deviled eggs and even called his *the best*.

As he glanced over the stove, he saw the eggs were occasionally bumping to each other as the water boiled. He set the timer and added his pre-measured splash of vinegar.

"Yes," he replied to all of it. "I'm bringing the eggs. I'll be there at five."

"Good. Do you have enough eggs for everyone?" she asked him. How many deviled eggs did she think people really needed?

Once he'd assured her—several times, though he didn't know why that was necessary—that he was making enough, she let him hang up.

Christian turned away from the boiling pot, knowing it was fine. A glance at the microwave assured him the timer was set so he headed to the spare bedroom in his house.

He hadn't yet unpacked the boxes he'd stacked in here. His mother liked to imagine he had a hoarding problem, but as of right now, he had used well over ten percent of the items he stored. That number was far too high for actual "hoarding." Also, he needed some of the things right now.

If he could find them.

The first item on his list was the robotic dog. He was pretty sure where it was, and as he opened the first box, he was glad to see the expected items. Digging down, he found the dog where he'd left it. The remote was a little harder to locate and he wound up unpacking and repacking the whole box. He found the remote as well as three pairs of swim goggles.

Christian set all of it aside, putting the goggles he'd thought he'd lost with his other swim gear. He could go tonight after dinner. Swimming always calmed him down and he hadn't gone to the pool this morning.

Returning to the kitchen, he transferred the eggs into an ice bath, then resumed opening as many boxes as he could. He grabbed various items as he went and threw them into a plastic grocery bag. He told himself he wasn't doing this to impress the teacher.

Riley Zayat was a bit of a mystery. Her last name was clearly Middle Eastern and, from what he could tell by looking at her, so was her heritage. Riley wasn't a Middle Eastern name though. Not at all. She didn't have a Southern accent, but he couldn't quite place the accent she did have. By looking at her, he could tell she was self-confident, comfortable with everyone he'd seen her interact with, and more than capable of taking charge of a situation. What he couldn't tell by looking at her was whether or not she found him attractive the same way he found her attractive.

She had wide, dark eyes and sleek hair that fell in waves to her shoulders. It shouldn't have looked that shiny at the end of a day with elementary students, but it did. She wore teacher clothes, but a little on the funky side and he wondered what she would wear if she wasn't at work. But she looked him in the eyes, answered all his questions, and had that ready smile.

He liked that she didn't look at him as though he made missteps in the conversation. She carried intelligent conversation and when he spoke about his work, she followed it. That was another oddity.

Most people understood when he explained what his app did. When he explained *how* he made the app, he lost them. He'd generally stopped explaining it. But Riley had asked. So he told her, fully expecting her to drop out of the conversation.

"It's a base program for general matching apps. I mean it could be applied to a dating site, but I intended for it to be broader use."

She nodded, not dropping out of the conversation at all. "So if I had a rare disease, it could match me to doctors in my area? Or if I wanted a particular food or a specific worker?"

"Like that, but I didn't write that. So you couldn't just go plug that in."

"Oh! So I can't buy your app in the app store."

He smiled, pleased when he didn't need to explain further.

"I would buy your app if I was a company?" He nodded and she continued. "Let's say I run a local support group for people with rare diseases. I would buy it and say what to match and your program would do it."

"Exactly." He'd not been able to hide the smile.

"Do you sell it directly to companies?"

He shook his head but before he could answer she jumped in. "You sold it... to a company that matches your app to places they can sell it. That's a little ironic."

Christian had felt his mouth quirk. No one had put it to him that way before. "I suppose it is. I get royalties when it sells."

Riley's expressive face said she was impressed. Or he thought it did. He wanted to believe it did.

He'd watched her run her classroom like a pro, too. Where he struggled, she excelled. She talked to each child differently, he'd noticed. She never made faces at any of them, no matter how strange or bizarre their questions or answers.

It was a job that appeared to him to be more difficult than herding cats. The kids didn't knock things off of tables like cats either; it was worse. The kids tried to make things that would spark and start a fire. They wanted to bring live animals into the classroom and let them loose. And they told each other truths that could be hurtful.

That was one issue Christian understood. His mother had gotten on his case for that more often than not. What he'd eventually learned was *just don't tell people*.

He'd spent most of his life not fitting in. While he wasn't comfortable being an adult in Riley's classroom, he thought he might have enjoyed being a kid there.

With his bag finally full of the things he'd dug up, he put it on the counter and put the robot dog and its remote into another bag. He labeled each and started a list of things he wanted to get, telling himself again that he wasn't trying to impress the teacher.

Besides, there wasn't much chance of that. He would have to remember to take the things on Wednesday, and he might screw that up. It wasn't his strong suit. He put both bags in the back of his car, just to be ready.

After he'd made the eggs and laid them out on the deviled egg plate his mother had given him for just such a purpose, he covered all of it in plastic wrap and headed over to Sunday dinner. It wasn't his favorite thing, but it wasn't the worst either.

His father opened the front door even before he could turn the knob. With a slap on his shoulder, his dad said, "Chris. Glad to have you back."

Christian had never been quite sure why his father agreed to his full name if he was only ever going to call him *Chris* but he'd stopped asking about that years ago.

Smiling for his dad, he headed into the house, as he knew what to do. Placing the deviled eggs in the middle of the table, he grabbed a small napkin. He piled it with the other appetizers —and several of his deviled eggs—and joined his cousin Jackson.

Jackson's young daughters, Scarlet and Salem, were running around the room singing a Disney song that Christian found obnoxious. But he didn't have the heart to tell the girls to stop. Jackson seemed to have tuned it out but that wasn't a skill Christian possessed.

He often didn't know how to talk to Jackson even though he wished he could. Jax's job as a cop was so foreign to Christian that he didn't even know where to start, so he usually didn't. Jax asked his usual question, "Where is Charlie this week?"

Christian wondered why everybody seemed to think he would always know where his brother was. But at least it was something to say. "Charlie's in Africa right now."

Christian explained his brother's whereabouts as best he knew, until the girls ran by again, their raised arms spread out as though they were airplanes. They were singing about snow, and Christian was confused.

Trying to tune them out again, he let his thoughts turn back to Riley, though he shouldn't, not until he had a better idea of how she felt. It was Jackson who turned to him again trying to start a conversation. "Are Scarlett and Salem twins because your brother and sister are twins? Does it run in the family that way?"

Christian shook his head. Normally, this wasn't his area of expertise, but he did know this about twins. When his parents told him that the younger sibling he was getting was actually *two* younger siblings, he'd learned everything he could on the topic. He'd known more about fetal twin development than any kid who didn't understand sex should.

He dug into that old, old knowledge now. "Charlie and Carlisle are fraternal twins. That generally runs maternally, so they got that from my mom. Your girls got their twinship from Shelle. Also, they're identical. It's a different phenomena."

Jackson's smile told him, *Thank you,* but he was obviously digesting the information. Christian considered continuing on with what he knew but remembered three facts was a good limit. So he shut up. His mother came around the corner then, filling the lull in the conversation. "Christian! How's your work going in Riley's classroom?"

He felt the heat flare in his face as he thought of Riley Zayat, and he turned to find his whole family looking at him.

✺ 5 ✺

Thursday of the following week, Riley watched as Christian came into the classroom.

On Wednesday, he'd walked in after the children were already there but didn't balk as they swarmed him. He seemed much more at ease.

"Hello, Molly. Hi, Jacee. Lisa Lynn, did you decide what you wanted to do?" He listened to the little girl's response and told her he could make that happen. "Hello, Marcus."

He stunned Riley by greeting each child by name.

He'd seen three different classes on three different days last week and he'd obviously been out of his element. But here he was, saying hello to each one by name as though he understood the children would notice if he left one out. He got them all correct.

Maybe he'd just needed to know how he fit in or know that the children weren't a pack of piranhas, but now he sat on the ground and pulled the robot dog out of the bag for Molly. Though he jerked back a little when Molly squealed, it didn't stop him from showing her all the parts. When Marcus tapped him on the arm, Christian startled again but covered nicely, including the boy in the conversation. "Here's the remote. And here's the port to hook it into the computer."

She was opening her mouth to say she didn't have a cable but she'd find one, when he pulled one out of the bag. "Here's the right cable. I checked your computers for the correct input."

He had?

As Riley watched, he plugged the dog into the computer and left Molly with a few simple instructions. While he worked with the other kids, Molly figured out how to make the dog sit, take a few steps, and play her favorite song.

It was not what Riley would have done. She would *not* have left Molly alone with such expensive equipment. But again, Christian had simply stated "I can fix it."

He'd next sat on the floor with Devon and showed him how the old phone worked. Then, at the end of the day, after she and he had finished and sent the children back to their homerooms, each with the beginning of a project in their head, he quietly checked out the dog. He tapped on the computer keyboard and appeared to clean off a few strange programs that Molly had created.

"Look what she did." He pointed to the screen, his voice wry. "She wrote a remote pattern to make the dog walk. I didn't see it work, but it's a good start. She's ready for another level of programming. Next week, we'll get that pattern functioning. We need to make it walk first. Then she can figure out how to make it run. That's an entirely different ballgame for a robot."

Riley had just smiled and thanked him. She thought it might mean more to buy him a coffee or something—but when she turned back around she saw he'd packed up the dog and placed it in its new spot on the shelf. Christian was already gone.

Today, he'd showed up with another bag of things he'd brought for the kids, and once again greeted each child by name. This class had three kids who wanted to look at some kind of gadgetry, robotics, or programming that Christian would help with. He'd said yes to all of them.

Sitting on the floor, he handed Liam a small screwdriver and then turned over the clock. "Now, what do we need to do to get this apart?"

Once all the kids agreed, Liam pulled out the screws. Christian handed them to Mitchell for safe keeping and asked Ellie to pull the alarm clock apart. It didn't work. Riley was having a tough time staying focused on the sewing machine Westerley Weaver had donated to the room for Jacob's project.

Though Riley was showing Jacob how to use the buttonhole setting, she was listening in as Christian explained that—despite the screws—many alarm clocks were glued shut. He pulled out a small hammer and handed it to Seven. Riley held her breath, then focused on helping Jacob decide if the buttonhole he'd stitched was large enough.

Behind her, the kids discussed what might be in the clock and how to get it open without damaging what they needed to steal. Christian next brought out an old radio. After assigning the jobs to different children this time, he showed them how it was different from the clock. Lastly, they opened an old tape player.

"Hey! It wasn't glued!" Melissa called out.

"Why is that?" he asked her and waited until one of the kids answered it.

"Is it old?" Seven asked.

But Christian frowned in response, at last asking the group, "What do you think?"

After they'd taken the units apart, he got all four kids logged into computers or tablets playing a simple game he'd found online that taught them fundamentals of coding. He finally took a step back and watched, answering questions when the kids got frustrated and basically untangling their errors.

It was then Riley noticed Lisa Lynn sitting quietly in her chair, frustrated.

He'd been doing so well, and clearly out of his comfort zone, too, but he didn't seem to notice the little girl. Riley's heart broke for her. Lisa Lynn would suffer in silence rather than ask for help. Riley was still angry that she'd only found out a month ago that the child's parents had an ugly split four months earlier. Lisa Lynn needed every bit of support she could get.

Leaving Jacob sewing and Carter researching pond microbes, she headed over to see what was wrong. Lisa Lynn answered with tears and a small finger pointing at the screen. "I can't make it work, Miss Zayat. Every time I try to make the turtle turn left, he turns *three times,* which is the same as *turning right*! I don't know what I did wrong!" She was in a full wail by the end.

Unfortunately, Riley didn't know what she'd done wrong either and she waved Christian over. As he came to stand behind the tiny chair, Riley noticed Lisa Lynn sinking ever so slightly downward. She was not Christian's biggest fan and Riley was about to find out why.

Lisa Lynn looked between the two of them for a moment, but then Christian said, "It's this," and pointed to the screen. "You can't put a period here."

"But that's where it goes. That's proper grammar. I learned it in class." Lisa Lynn countered, stubbornness shining.

"No," Christian told her, as always straightforward and honest. Maybe he was being a bit too technical for an overly sensitive fourth grader, though. Riley decided she would stay and be a buffer

"But I have to do the sentences right! I did them right!"

"It's not the same language," Christian told the girl. "The grammar you're using is for English. Computers don't speak English. Look at your code."

Lisa Lynn did, but she didn't smile. She didn't seem to see an answer.

"You told it all the right things to do," he said to her, "But you told it in a mix of code and English. You have to just use code."

"But it is English. That's English. *That's English!*" She was getting more and more frustrated.

Riley wanted to step in. She wanted to soothe ruffled feathers and stop Christian before he got angry with a child who was getting too worked up to listen.

At least he didn't rise to the bait and stayed calm. But he said the same thing. "No, it's not English. It's C-plus."

"Actually," she hopped in, "code was created by English speakers in many cases. And so in many cases, the code uses English words. But Mr. Weaver is correct. It's not actually the same language. And you can continue putting English grammar in it, but I think your turtle will continue doing the wrong thing. Why don't we try it Mr. Weaver's way and let's see what happens?"

It took a few more minutes trying to decide if Christian should take the keyboard and simply fix it or just explain it and let Lisa Lynn figure it out. Riley voted hard for the second option but forced herself to stay back.

When the turtle at last turned left the appropriate number of times, Lisa Lynn smiled up at him and said, "Thank you, Mr. Weaver," as though nothing had ever been wrong.

Soon, the turtle was not only turning correctly, he also wiggled his butt exactly as she had programmed. Next, he ran off the screen, making the little girl giggle and Christian smile. Even Riley had to get in on that one. But it was getting late and the children had to go back to their regular classrooms. So once again, she stopped them and had them spend their last fifteen minutes cleaning up.

She was shocked when Christian stopped Seven on the way out the door.

"I'm glad you did the programming today," he told the boy. "I know you wanted to make toys and gadgets, but we need to do the programming a little bit first. Next week we can start putting some pieces together."

Riley hadn't quite caught on that that's why Seven had done the work at the computer station but hadn't been quite as enthusiastic as the others. It was a good catch on Christian's part, and as Seven left he brightened up. Still, he turned to Christian and said, "I watched James Bond last week and I want to be like Q."

"Oh," Christian replied. "I don't know Q, but I'll see what I can do."

Seven then proceeded to skip down the hallway and Riley watched. Once Seven was almost out of sight, she came back into the room to find Christian was already closing down programs. Once again, he tapped the keys as though cleaning out anything the kids might have done that would leave behind problems. Riley could clear her cache and delete her passwords, but that was the extent of her skills. She was grateful he was easily stepping up and doing all the peripheral work that went with kids, too.

She was getting ready to ask again if she could take him for a coffee when he turned and said, "I read up on the teaching methods you mentioned. The Socratic Method looked like the best fit, but it was really hard."

Her mouth must have flown open into an O. "You read up on teaching methods?"

He nodded at her.

"How much?"

"I looked up Montessori, and Walden, and Socratic Method. I tried to find some childhood development information about these ages." He was still looking at her as though she was the one who was nuts.

"And you thought Socratic Method was best?"

He frowned at her. "Are you using it on me now?"

"Oh, God, no!" Of course, she had asked a handful of stupid questions right after he told her he was using a questions-only teaching method. "I'm not. I'm just so surprised that you went to all the effort." Then, she finally got the words out of her mouth. "Can I buy you a coffee? Maybe an afternoon snack? We can talk somewhere outside this classroom."

She smiled and hoped he'd say yes. She was now fascinated that he'd been researching this project.

But he only stuttered and said, "Tomorrow?"

❧ 6 ❧

"No," Riley protested. "*Please,* let me buy the coffee."

"It's okay." Christian countered her, in that way he did that was deep-ocean calm. Even when he was telling her "no." "I don't mind."

"But I do. *I* asked *you* out for coffee. Besides, you've showed up each day in my classroom with a bag of presents for the children." Riley stepped forward in the line, still fighting for her right to pay as the line moved slowly. He'd come out with her, having no qualms climbing into a car with her. Men often did, as though if they couldn't be the driver, they couldn't go. But Christian only said he didn't know where they were going, and readily agreed. She continued her battle. "I understand. The first two days, you brought things that you already owned. But you showed up today with four brand new programmable motherboards. I have a hard time believing that you just had those lying around your house."

As she said it, she realized Christian was the person most likely to actually have that. She watched his expression for a sign and, sure enough, he gave it. He had no poker face. He was just as easy to read as he was to look at. Christian glanced off to the side as they stepped up another space in line at the coffee shop.

Riley laughed. "Don't even try to tell me you already had those. They were still in the cardboard boxes!"

He looked off to the side again.

Riley smiled at him when he finally looked back at her. His return smile set off a flutter, which she viciously tamped down. Despite asking him out for coffee, she couldn't afford to get involved with this man. For a million reasons.

He was her class helper and she needed him. He was town royalty—his mother a Mayfair in a town that had once been named after the family. And she was just someone who came to work in the town because her grandparents lived here. She wasn't a Southern Belle, not fit for the likes of Christian Weaver, even if circumstances had lined up. So she told him, "You're not that good a liar. I know you bought those for the kids."

"It seemed like it was a really good thing for the kids."

"Oh, it is." She found herself smiling again. He made her do that a lot. "It's fantastic." As soon as they ordered, she handed over her credit card to pay for two coffees and pastries. That he ordered a black coffee at a place known for all the frou-frou extras didn't surprise her. His just-as-easy order of a chocolate croissant did. When they found a clear table and sat down, she decided she had to make things clear. "I just want to be sure you understand that I don't expect you to fund the program."

He nodded. "It just seemed easier to do what I need to do if I have the proper equipment."

"We could order it," she said, but it was an empty offer. He'd already bought the expensive pieces. The school might pay for one or two of the programmable boards but not four. There would be red tape, so much red tape. The pieces might not arrive until February. But she held all of this back.

"This was faster," he offered as though he understood the problems she faced, as though it was no problem at all to spend the money on her kids.

"I appreciate it. Which is why I'm getting you coffee."

She liked Christian Weaver but quickly reminded herself it

didn't matter. She couldn't afford to lose her computer guy. Couldn't afford to disappoint the kids. Besides, she was fully involved in his family now. His mother came on Mondays and Tuesdays, and she wouldn't take kindly to Riley developing feelings for her son. Would she? Also, his cousin Bailey Ann volunteered. Her father was dying, her mother already gone, with Bailey left as the sole caretaker. Westerley had pitched Bailey Ann as a bit of a charity case. The woman had turned out to be anything but. Again, anything with Christian might interfere with her other relationships.

Not worth the risk. Riley told herself. *Her kids were everything.*

"Riley!" the barista called it out, startling both of them, but she hopped up and fetch their order. As soon as everything was laid out and she took the first sip of her fully doctored brew the conversation stilted a little. So she went and put her foot in it.

"Can I ask you a question?" she asked as though she had a right to. "Have you been tested? Are you on the autism spectrum?"

His eyes blinked at her and she realized as soon as she said it, that it was wholly inappropriate. *What had she done? She should have just kissed him.*

"No," he replied still ocean-calm. Only this time she thought it masked a storm coming, and she realized she'd screwed up on several levels. That deep-sea calm when he clearly wasn't emotionless was one of the things that made her think that maybe he was on the spectrum. She'd suspected he had what they would have once called Asperger's Syndrome.

His literal interpretation of questions was definitely a flag. So she tried to step a little more carefully this time. "I'm sorry, that was a crappy question."

"It's okay." He started to cut the croissant with a knife and fork but then looked around the store. She followed his gaze, not knowing what he was searching for. But he set down the utensils and started to peel the pastry.

Watching him, Riley did the same. At first it was to make

him more comfortable. But after a bite, she realized she really got the layers of a croissant when it was peeled. After another moment's silence, she tried again, but with a little more tact and better questions. "No, I can't ask? No, you haven't been tested? Or no, you have been tested but you're not on the spectrum?"

"You can ask," he said, and popped another peeled layer of pastry into his mouth. He didn't seem upset that she'd brought it up. "And I have been tested, and the test said I wasn't."

She nodded, trying to channel some of his reserve, even though his answer surprised her.

Christian looked at her, his eyes narrowing a little. "You think that's wrong."

"Do you?" she tossed back, only then realizing he might wonder if she was using the Socratic Method on him again.

He thought about it for a moment, the expression on his face making her wonder if he'd never questioned it himself, but when he spoke, he said, "Maybe."

"I'm sorry," she apologized again. "I shouldn't have asked."

"It's okay. It's a legitimate question and maybe the test was wrong."

And that was such an ASD answer that she wanted to tell him, *Yes. Yes, it was.*

"Does it make me weird?" he asked as he stopped peeling the pastry. He'd reached the river of chocolate down the middle and was now using the knife and fork again.

Riley threw back her head and laughed. "Please! We're all weird. Have you seen my kids? You met me. I'm weird. No, it just gives a framework. That's all. Weird is good."

The light in his eyes when she said that made her think about why she'd gone into this line of work. They were here, in the coffee shop, and she didn't have anything else she *needed* to tell him. So she started talking. "When I was a kid, I almost flunked reading class. Never mind that I had been reading Stephen King at the age of six. That I read The Once and Future

King before I was out of second grade. I read all of the Clan of the Cave Bear series by third."

"So why did you flunk reading? That seems advanced."

"Yes, I flunked because I didn't read the books in class, so I couldn't pass the tests on them. And no one looked to see that I *was* reading. While I was very good at reading and math, I was terrible with tech." Riley sighed, wondering if Christian could even relate to that. "Anything they put in my hands, I messed up. I always did the wrong thing. None of it was intuitive to me. Now, I feel lucky. I can use my phone without it hanging up every time I try to make a call. I text the wrong person all the time."

He laughed. "Phones are easy. They're just computers. A phone does exactly what it's told to do."

"Sure, sure." She knew that. "But apparently I don't speak the same language it does."

That made him nod and think a little bit, and she appreciated that he didn't just tell her she was doing it wrong. She turned the conversation a bit. "You're great at all things school oriented but not so social."

Christian nodded. "That's correct. I didn't fit in anywhere."

"Maybe that's because you skipped a grade." Riley held out an olive branch that maybe it hadn't been his fault. His willingness to dive in was endearing. Though she wasn't certain why she found it necessary to make him comfortable with that, she did. "Right in the middle of high school, too. That doesn't help anything."

"I also skipped third grade," he said between bites, throwing it out as casually as if he'd said he saw a dog go by the window.

Riley felt her mouth fall open. "That's a lot for one kid."

He shrugged. "To be fair, I don't think I would have fit in better if I'd stayed in my original grade."

"We won't know now," she said. "But these days, we work very hard not to skip kids for exactly that reason. We try not to make kids deal with the kinds of things you had to deal with. It must have been hard always being the youngest and the smartest."

"Smart is different in different people." He offered, his plate clean but the coffee not yet empty. "I don't read people very well, but you do a really good job with that."

"Thank you, but it was something I had to learn. I worked really hard at being a good teacher and I see other teachers who just automatically know what to do with the kids. I pay a lot of attention. I try to figure out who's acting what way and if it's different from their normal behavior. If they're acting out or acting poorly, I ask *is there something causing it?* I constantly have to remind myself to check. It doesn't feel intuitive to me. Math feels intuitive. Running all the special classes for the kids? That feels intuitive. It feels like exactly what I was made to do. I love watching the kids and I love when I get it right, but I work really hard at that."

He looked at her a little sideways then and she wondered if he was thinking maybe he could learn to work at it too. Maybe he could.

"You do a very good job." He pushed the plate away, finished with it. "Your hard work pays off."

"Thank you." Then she moved the subject away from herself. "You're fitting in very well with my class. The kids all love you and the ones who are working with you are getting so far. I can't thank you enough for volunteering."

He looked off to the side again and Riley caught it. It was one of the things she always watched for in her kids and it was easy to spot on this man. She sighed. "You didn't volunteer, did you?"

He shook his head. "Not really. My mother and I were talking, and she told me all about your class. I said it sounded wonderful, because it did. I didn't realize Mom was setting me up. You would think I'm old enough now to know when my mother is setting me up. But I missed it."

Riley couldn't help but smile. "She Vollun-told you, didn't she?"

"Pretty much."

This time, it was Riley who looked off to the side. "Christian," she said and waited until she caught his gaze. "You don't have to come back. I'm sure you have other projects that you're working on, and we'll figure out a workaround. I'm sorry. I thought you had actually wanted to come work with the class. I thought you had *volunteered*."

He blinked two or three times and didn't say anything while Riley waited it out. She was going to lose him. Holding her breath, she hoped for a better outcome.

"Are you trying to get rid of me? I can go if you think it's not working."

God, this man was always a surprise.

"Oh, no. It's wonderful. I love having you in the classroom." As the words flew out of her mouth, she realized how much they were true.

7

Christian looked at his mother. She'd asked what he wanted for his birthday this year.

He was blindsided by her question, just as he always was. *Shit*. It was going into November. He should have known. She asked every year, and every year he wasn't ready.

She wanted a short list of things that she could provide for his birthday, something different from what he got for Christmas. She said he was hard to buy for, that she didn't know enough about the things he liked to pick them out. Westerley Mayfair Weaver had a hard line against gift cards. She said they showed you didn't know the person well enough to get a real gift. But Christian always wondered why simply asking what to get him wasn't the same thing.

And he didn't have a ready answer to her question.

Unfortunately, what he always wanted for his birthday was to not be born on Christmas Day, and that wasn't anything anyone could provide, even his mother.

He was a grown man. He should have gotten over all the years that his birthday was celebrated with his parents and his younger siblings and not with friends and not with a party. Not that he had many friends, and not that he knew how to throw a party, but that had always been his goal.

He remembered wanting a table in the back yard with a shiny plastic cloth. Treats laid out at each seat. Cake for everyone and presents from everyone. Instead, his birthday had always been a side note on a huge family holiday.

He couldn't tell his mother that; it would hurt her feelings. So he went with his golden rule and didn't say anything. Instead, a new answer came to him quickly. "I think I'd like a couple of those remote-controlled robots that you can buy off the shelf at one of the electronics stores."

Her face went wide, her words confirming that she disbelieved his ready answer. "Just a minute ago, you looked like you didn't have an answer for me at all. But there you go with this. And it's very specific."

He shrugged as she looked at him again, with more scrutiny. "What do you want with robots? You can build better ones than that."

That was true, and he didn't have time for a lie. "It'd be great for Riley's classroom."

He saw the expression in her eyes and knew he had said something that made her think something. He shouldn't have said "Riley," he should have said, "Miss Zayat." But quick social thinking and masking his thoughts was not in his wheelhouse. But his mother looked like she was still thinking and he had no idea *what* she was thinking.

"So you like it there, at the classroom?"

"It has its benefits. But Mom, I don't need you volunteering me for other things," he chastised her.

"You didn't have anything to do," she protested. Defending her Mom-ness as she always did. Mostly when he didn't need her doing whatever Mom-thing she'd done. "You needed something to fill your time and I had a place that needed you."

"Just because I didn't have anything marked on my calendar didn't mean I didn't have anything to do."

At that, she looked genuinely distraught. "I'm sorry. I didn't realize... Did you? Did this interrupt something you need to be doing?"

Fuck. Now he was forced to admit it. "No, I didn't. I was looking for one, but I didn't have one already. I can find my own work, though."

She definitely changed the topic. Though he watched her do it, he couldn't have said *how* she did it, and he couldn't have repeated the practice for himself.

"So what do you think of Riley Zayat?"

He shrugged, having learned a while ago that a shrug was a good way to avoid a question. Unfortunately, it didn't work on his mother.

"Tell me."

"She's nice," he said, trying for Riley's most innocuous feature. He didn't mention her ready smile, or the way her eyes lit up when she saw him. It was the same when she saw the children, so he was sure he wasn't special to her. Didn't mean he didn't like it though. "She's really good with the children."

He didn't add that he was jealous of the kids. Didn't say, *It would have been nice to have a teacher like Riley Zayat when I was a kid.* If he had a teacher like her, he would have been head over heels in love with her.

His mother looked at him through narrowed eyes then and he remembered the way his face had heated when everyone asked about Riley at Sunday dinner. He told himself he wouldn't say more. But then the words fell out of his mouth. "She's always figuring out what each one of them needs."

His mother agreed as she sipped her tea, "She's very intuitive with those children."

"No, she's not," he corrected, startling his mother.

"She's great with the kids!" Westerley Weaver argued back, and he liked that his mother was defending Riley.

"She is *great* with the kids, Mom, but she's not *intuitive*. She told me she works very hard at it. She watches carefully and counts all their behaviors. And when the behaviors change, she tries to figure out what made it change. It's very data driven."

"Hmm," his mother said. That was a sound that meant something was coming. Though he knew that, he'd still never learned how to predict *what* was coming.

"Did she tell you that?" His mother's head tilted. He could tell she was ferreting information, but Christian wasn't good enough at that game to know what to give and what to hide.

So he just said, "Yes."

When Westerley pushed, he had to give up more. "The other day, she took me out for coffee to thank me."

His mother hmmmm-ed again, and he tried to ignore it.

When they finished their lunch, Christian put all their trash into the bin and was turning to hug her goodbye. This was a normal thing for them, going out to lunch. She seemed to enjoy taking him out. Maybe she just enjoyed feeding people. Or maybe it was as if she thought he would eat nothing but chips and soda all week.

He couldn't fault her; that had happened more than once.

But she stepped away from his hug. "Let's go next door. We can walk right over and get those robots."

Well, that wasn't what he'd planned to do next. But she seemed to want to go. It wasn't even really what he wanted for his birthday. He wanted a real birthday present. He wanted it wrapped up and presented on his birthday at a party, but he was willing to settle for the robots.

When he offered his best forced-smile, she really looked at him and raised one eyebrow as though to challenge his suggestion. "If you want it for the class, let's get it for the class. That means as soon as possible."

He almost protested. Riley had told him to stop bringing things. To stop spending money for the class. Instead, he followed his mother out the door and through the brisk air. He walked beside her across the parking lot to where the blue and yellow store sat waiting to provide them with several toy robots.

In the end his mother bought four, protesting that she'd never paid for his college. The least she could do was make his classroom happy.

Christian thought about that. It wasn't *his* classroom. It was *Riley's*. And Riley was going to protest that he was bringing more new expensive toys.

But he liked that the robots would make her happy. And she couldn't say no, he thought. After all, *he* hadn't bought them.

❧ 8 ❧

There are 12 acceptable silver patterns, not that this matters. You inherit your pattern.

RILEY SET OUT HER NICEST SILVER ONTO FOLDED CLOTH napkins and placed three of her wine glasses on the patio table. It was one of the few very warm days in the middle of the cooling fall. It had sprung up randomly between cold, wind, and rain, but today there was seventy-degree sun.

Georgia was just like that, she had learned. While it didn't make any sense, she was certainly going to take advantage of it. Bailey Ann Mayfair was right behind her with two plates in her hands. Angelia Fortney, a fellow teacher at Brighton and a good friend, followed along with the third plate of a chicken dish Riley's grandmother had given her the recipe for. Riley had served it up with potatoes—because this was the *South*.

Bailey Ann contributed the salad—and not one of the jello variety, which Riley had learned was an actual thing around here. Angelia supplied two bottles of her favorite sparkling blanc de blancs. One bottle was still stashed in the fridge, but the other was tucked up under her arm.

"It's really beautiful outside for this. I'm glad we got together tonight." Bailey Ann put down the plates and reached out to help Riley.

"I'm glad you came over. It was a whole week of little kids and a side helping of parents." Riley sighed. "Thank God it's Friday."

"I had two melt downs to deal with," Angelia offered.

"I had a kid try to set my room on fire." Riley thought about Lisa Lynn deciding she wanted to be just like Christian and tried to rewire the radio.

"I had my father fight me over his meds," Bailey Ann joined in.

It felt good to be getting things off their chests. All three were doing what they loved, but nothing came without challenges. Riley added with a wry twist, "And I had three volunteers to coordinate."

That at least made Bailey smile, as she was one of those volunteers. Then she tipped her head. "How's Christian working out for you? He's a little... odd."

Riley almost laughed out loud. "I teach the *gifted class,*" she reminded them. "*Odd* is my bread and butter and, no, your cousin doesn't really qualify. He's too smart."

This time it was Bailey Ann who laughed as she pulled the cork on the bottle and poured generous servings in each glass. "Smart doesn't mean not odd. I think he's smarter than all the rest of us put together, but he never really did quite get the hang of social interactions. It might be because of all those skipped grades." She recorked the wine and picked her glass up for a sip. "Might be because he's so smart. Might be because he's odd."

Angelia pulled out one chair, scraping the metal legs across the patio. It was a sound that would have driven Riley crazy except it meant she was eating out on the back deck. Seating herself, she dove back into defending Christian. "I actually think he may be on the autism spectrum scale. Not by much—but he does a few things that made me think that might be the case."

"Interesting," Bailey Ann drew the word out as she set down her wine glass.

As soon as Riley had said it though, she felt the need to add, "A lot of us fit the scale someplace or other. Doesn't mean we actually have ASD." But then she began to wonder which part of what she'd said Bailey Ann found interesting, so she asked, "Did you never think that he might be on the spectrum?"

"It's not that," Bailey answered. "It's that you're defensive of him."

Riley felt her face flush hot and there was nothing she could do to stop it.

"Oh, my God." Bailey Ann raised her wine glass, indicating that Riley should clink it in a toast. Angelia followed suit and chimed her glass against the other two, even though Riley wasn't quite sure what they were toasting yet. Angelia cleared it up.

"It appears that Miss Zayat has a crush on Mr. Weaver," her voice singsonged, then she took a big gulp in celebration.

"Oh," Riley shook her head. "No, no, that's not what's happening."

Her friends shared a look between them, and Riley couldn't help but know what it meant.

Angelia made the effort to say it. "I think she doth protest too much."

There was nothing to do but shut her mouth. It didn't work. She *tried* to stop talking, but words came out anyway. "It doesn't matter what I think. I can't get involved with him. He's a volunteer in my classroom."

It was Bailey Ann who turned to Angelia and asked, "Miss Fortney, is there a rule about volunteers and teachers fraternizing?"

Riley was protesting, "Do *not* try to set me up—"

But the other two women were paying no attention to her.

"Why no, Bailey Ann. There's *not* a rule about that," Angelia replied with a smile, her glass still raised before she took another deep drink, as though already toasting a new relationship.

Riley rolled her eyes. "It's not happening," she told them and took a bite of her chicken. "Oh my god. That's good."

She wasn't sure if she said it because the chicken was so good —it was—or maybe she'd said it to change the subject. It worked, but she wasn't fooling anyone. She knew that.

"I haven't ever had a dish quite like this." Angelia was cutting into her chicken and Riley was pleased to see it disappearing. Usually that was a good sign.

Bailey Ann shook her head in agreement. This was more how Riley had pictured her little end-of-the-week get-together on the back patio. She'd not expected a set up or for her friends to gang up on her. Then again, the other two had known each other for longer than she had. So maybe it was her own fault for not seeing it coming. She'd expected to talk about school, about Bailey Ann's dad's health, and about the chicken.

"It's my grandmother's recipe, a Middle Eastern dish." One that normally didn't pair with Southern potatoes, but Riley had done it anyway.

"Well, it's fabulous," Angelia said as she took another bite.

They were partway through the meal when Riley had to ask, "Bailey, why do you keep looking at the silver?"

"Oh, I just don't recognize the pattern. I thought I recognized *all* the old silver patterns."

"Ah," Riley replied. "That's because I'm not a belle like you two. So it's not real silver. It's plated. In fact, it's what they call 'gas station silver.'"

Bailey Ann's mouth fell open and Angelia's brows pulled together. "What's 'gas station silver'?"

Bailey Ann got herself together and said, "Oh my god, you've got *gas station silver.*"

Well, at least one of them knew what it was, Riley thought. But it was Bailey Ann who explained it to Angelia. "Several generations ago, instead of earning points for savings when you bought gas or things at the store, you got points and you could order out of a catalog. You could even save up enough points to get good china and plated silverware! It was real patterns and real china, but it was commonly known as *gas station silver*."

Bailey then examined the plate she was eating off and asked, "Do you have the china, too?"

Riley shook her head. "I got my own china. Picked it out myself at the outlet mall outside Alpharetta." It was new, and she'd been excited to get to use it tonight.

"Well, me too. I totally understand that one." Angelia added and Bailey Ann stayed out of that conversation. They pretty much all knew that Bailey Ann had inherited both her silver and her china from her grandmothers. It was the way belles did it.

But even as Riley was thinking that, Bailey Ann was frowning and looking at her oddly. "What do you mean you're not a belle?"

Even Angelia was looking at her like she was bonkers, though Riley thought it was obvious to anyone who looked. "Well, I didn't grow up in Breathless, or even in the south."

She was from Northern California and they both knew it. So why on earth would anyone think she was a belle?

Angelia popped in, "Your grandma was a belle. She lives here. Being a belle is passed down maternally. That makes you a belle."

"And you got her silver," Bailey Ann pointed out. "I think you qualify."

Riley just laughed. "It's gas station silver. And I'm Middle Eastern and Jewish. My name is Raizel Shoshana Zayat, and I grew up in Eureka, California."

Bailey Ann and Angelia looked at each other, quite confused. All at once, they spoke over each other.

"That doesn't make you not a belle," Angelia seemed flummoxed.

"Look at you," Bailey Ann piled on. "You've got fine china and silver. How many little black dresses do you own?"

"Three," Riley replied. It was almost a requisite number.

"My fiancé is from Ohio," Angelia added in. "Don't think that I'm not a belle anymore and don't think that my daughters won't be belles, too." She paused, "And I haven't ever told anybody, but my grandma's silver was plated, too."

Riley just laughed.

It was Bailey Ann's smile that did her in. "Belles aren't what you think. I mean, we used to be all white girls out of plantations. But the days of Tara are long over."

Angelia smiled. "Belles come in all sizes and colors and backgrounds now. Bailey Ann's aunt is black, and you can't tell anyone that Aunt GiGi isn't a belle. She's more belle than me. And my Daddy's family has been here for five generations, but my Mama's from Ohio. She just fit right in and she's a belle now, too."

"It's about being able to hold up the sky when everything is falling. Belles ran the South during the war, you know. It's about having roots—whatever they are. And it's about loving the South. Real love, the kind that wants the south to grow, not the kind that's blind to her faults. It was three belles that organized that march in Atlanta, and you can't get anything past them!" Bailey Ann looked at Riley, then at Angelia. "I think she qualifies."

"Oh, yeah. She was a belle and didn't even know it."

Riley pressed her lips together, fighting the happy tears that wanted to come. It was amazing that these strong women thought that highly of her. She wasn't sure how much she bought it, but she did have her grandmother's silver. Raising her glass, she smiled. "I accept."

Angelia grinned and clinked her glass again. "Bring on the Middle Eastern chicken!"

Bailey joined in. "Amen, that's good! Oh, but girl, you've got to get yourself some drawl."

❧ 9 ❧

Two weeks later, Christian walked into Riley's classroom on a Thursday afternoon, smiling.

He noticed that entering the school didn't make him apprehensive anymore. He'd grown to feel comfortable here. He knew the children and they all knew him. They even seemed to like him.

He'd picked out a project at home, too. Between that and volunteering here and his mother making sure he showed up for every Sunday dinner, his time was getting full.

He was spending the bulk of his days working on making the app he had developed more specific. It wasn't difficult work, but it was definitely time consuming. Every tiny piece had to work no matter what the company needed. Input had to be accepted in many possible forms. It was both tedious and mentally challenging to fix everything he could think of, then think of more ways the average user might try to follow instructions incorrectly. The work was something he needed until he got his next big idea, because he hadn't gotten it yet.

"Hey, Christian." Riley looked up and smiled as he entered the classroom, her words like a starting gun to the tangle of small children who began screaming and yelling and basically acting like he was a rock star.

"Mr. Weaver, I made a play cell phone at home!"

"Mr. Weaver, I fixed my dad's toaster!"

"Mr. Weaver, I want to make a robot centipede. I brought a real one so we can use it for design."

Oh-kay, all was well until the little hands held up the dirty centipede and it moved like it was coming for him. Christian blinked.

Riley jumped in and simply took it from the child's hands. With a stern look, she asked, "What's our rule about bringing live animals in the classroom?"

Christian didn't hear the answer through his surprise that this must have happened often enough to make a rule about it. Still, the anxiety didn't come. Somehow, even all of this had become normal.

Though Riley had protested the four programmable robots he'd brought in earlier, Christian made her keep them. He'd handed them over and waited a beat for her to tell him that he shouldn't have. Sure enough, it was the first thing out of her mouth when she'd seen what was in the bag.

"Christian, you can't keep buying gifts like this for the classroom."

"But," he replied, "these aren't from me. They're from my mother." He'd smiled as she shook her head at him but had no good comeback. One simply did not turn down Westerley Weaver.

The next week, however, Riley came back to him. "So, I was talking to your mother and thanking her for her kind gift..."

Uh oh, he thought. Though everything was on the up-and-up, he was certain this wasn't going to end the way he wanted.

"—and apparently, even though Mrs. Weaver purchased the robots, they were your birthday present." Riley was frowning at him, as though to ask, *how are you going to get out of this one?*

Christian didn't know, so he just shrugged.

Today he'd brought a hot plate.

Riley raised an eyebrow at him there, but he protested. "I'm taking it home when we're done. So don't even think I'm leaving these little Edisons with something they can burn things with."

She couldn't hold back the laugh though she clearly didn't know what to do with him. He wondered if he was keeping it to himself how much he'd come to love this volunteer position. He really liked working with the kids. Even more, he liked seeing Riley. Besides, she'd already given permission for him to bring the hotplate.

Seven came over to sit down next to him, pieces of his laser gun project in his hands. "Do we have all the pieces?"

"I think so," Christian replied. "Did you bring the plastics?"

Seven pulled handfuls of old broken shards of various items out of his pocket. It seemed he'd been collecting them for the whole week and just shoved them in there. To his credit, he had a good variety, including different colors, thicknesses, and softnesses.

"Oh, you should have put that in a plastic bag," Christian said, "We don't want it to cut you."

The little boy nodded. "Yeah, that makes sense. Ever would have said to put it in a plastic bag, but I didn't tell her. I just collected it."

Christian didn't know what the boy was talking about, but it didn't make a difference now. "Well, let's take a look through it."

Christian had the boy lay all the pieces out on one of the desks. They sorted all the varieties and matching pieces. Then they pulled the whole desk over near the wall, so the hotplate cord wouldn't dangle. He explained, "We don't want any screaming children trying to get from one project to another running by and getting caught in our cord."

"Well, yeah," Seven replied as though it were obvious. "Then you'd have a screaming kid because they got burned by a hot plate."

Christian couldn't argue with that, so he just said, "Safety first," and positioned everything where he figured no one would burn themselves. Then he plugged in the hot plate and prayed. "The first thing we need to do is test these. You've got several pieces of most of the kinds of plastic."

"Not these two," Seven told him and pulled those aside.

"Okay, we can't use those because we can't test them. Does that make sense?"

Seven nodded and scooped up the two pieces tucking them back into his pocket. Even as he did it, Riley came by and said, "Here's a bag. Let's keep them inside for safety."

Christian grinned up at her from where he sat in the elementary school chair. That wasn't very sexy of him, he knew, but he didn't have much game anyway. Riley didn't have children of her own, but she definitely reminded him of a mom the way she was constantly swooping in and taking care of things, preventing problems before they even occurred.

"All right." He held up one of the smaller pieces of plastic in front of Seven. "I'm going to do the first one, just to show you how. Then—if you're safe—you can do the others."

He held the plastic over the now warm hot plate and let it get gooey. He watched the boy's eyes grow wide. "Okay, now we're going to put these together."

Christian touched the molten plastic onto another sample piece they had, letting it dry and harden in a weld. Once it was done, he said, "We're going to do three or four more, and then we'll test them."

Together, they melted more plastic bits and pushed the pieces together. Seven worked diligently and carefully, much to Christian's delight. Riley didn't once have to swoop in and save them. Once the pieces were cool, he gave Seven the job of trying to break them back apart.

They found two that were difficult to break.

"Those are our choices," Christian pointed out.

"Let's use this one." Seven pointed to the one he liked. Though Christian was waiting for a comment on the thickness of the plastic or that it had bonded quickly, Seven said, "Orange is cool."

So they melted the pieces down bit by bit and used an old plastic squirt gun they'd chopped the top off of. Using the melted plastic, they bonded it to the flashlight base they'd used for their laser pointer. Christian smiled. They were getting close to making James Bond toys. When at last they had the laser pointer mounted where the barrel of the gun would have gone, Seven's breath sucked in.

"Whoa! That looks wicked!" He held the gun up and pulled the trigger. Then he pulled it again, and again as his frown deepened.

Christian laughed at the little boy's frustration. "Nothing works unless we make it work. That's our next job—line up the trigger with the button."

"Yes," Seven smiled, but most of the afternoon was gone. "Is that our job for next week?"

Christian nodded, because even though class wasn't over, he needed to help Ellie. She'd changed her project to a computer code program. Her hope was to build a game each of the other kids could play.

He'd set the kid up with a story board last week, and Ellie had come in today with it almost finished. Heading to the other side of the room, Christian looked at where the little girl was holding it up to show him, having just put the finishing touches on. He'd seen prettier storyboards in his day, but this was a valiant first effort.

"That's a really cool game you designed."

And that was right up his alley. So he had everything rolling, where Ellie was working on the preliminary code as he watched over her shoulder and checked it. He corrected errors, gave her a few tips and pointers, then assigned her next tasks. Ellie soaked it up like a sponge.

When the afternoon was finally over, the children left. In a few moments, the room went from full and noisy to calm and quiet. Suddenly, it was just him and Riley, cleaning up, as usual.

She always impressed him. While he was very attracted to her, he didn't know if it was wrong to date the woman he volunteered for. The last thing he wanted was to make her uncomfortable, but the first thing he wanted to do was to ask her out.

It probably didn't matter, because he sucked at it. He'd asked women out in the past and managed to do it in such a way that they didn't realize he meant "on a date." Or they just said No. Some were polite, some were less so, but no was no.

He told himself he didn't need to ask her out. That it was okay to just enjoy being around her. But the more he'd gotten to know Riley Zayat, the more he liked her. It wasn't just that she understood him. It was that she didn't even think he was odd. She sparked new ideas in him. Asked him questions about what he was doing and seemed genuinely interested in his answers. She took him for coffee once a week, but it was only a thank you... he thought.

She turned then, and looked right at him, surprising him with her insight. It was as though she knew he was thinking about her. Her question wasn't about him, though. "What do you think of Ellie's game?"

"I think she's got the basic hang of it. It's a simple game. But I think it could be used for other things."

"That's what I was thinking," Riley told him. "Honestly, I think if you could make it into a phone app, it could be used for kids on the autism spectrum. Or it could be for anybody."

"How would it be a phone app?"

"Not that game in particular. But the setup where you build your own game," she turned away, picked up a few things and organized a stack of papers while she talked.

Christian watched, but he was thinking, catching on to her idea. "So I would build the base platform."

"Like you do," she added in with a smile as though he was the only one capable of building a base platform for something.

"I have to finish the work that I contracted for SixCo before I can work on anything else."

"I don't think it matters when you do it." She was still picking up pieces of something from the floor and putting them in three separate places in the shelves. "I don't think there's any competition for a game like this. But I'd bet there's a lot of market for it."

He was thinking as he turned around and grabbed two of the robots from where several of the kids had been playing with them. One of them said "Christian" suddenly—in Riley's voice—as he picked it up. He tried not to show how startled he was. He should have known better than to give the kids a system that would record voices and play it back randomly.

He held one robot up toward Riley. "Watch out for this. When you get out the projector or the TV, those remotes work on the same radio frequencies that these do. Sometimes you can trigger the robot to say a word or start dancing just by changing the channel. It really freaks people out if they don't know what's going on."

Riley was grinning. "I can see where that would happen."

But she didn't add anything more, so he turned and put the robots away. He hadn't asked her out yet; he was waiting for the perfect opening but it never seemed to come. They worked a few more minutes in silence and at last there was nothing left for him to do.

She was watching him. Just like she'd told him she did with the kids, she was probably counting his actions and noticed he was out of character. "Is there something you need?"

"No." But he turned away feeling his face flash red. He waved his hand over his shoulder as he headed right out the door, once again not having asked her out.

❧ 10 ❧

Christian tapped at the tiny keyboard on his phone, anxiety getting the better of him.

—Carlisle. I need your help.

Her reply was quick, but not what he was hoping for.

—What on earth could you possibly need MY help for?

He was tapping away, typing out his answer. When a second reply popped up from his sister.

—OMG RU finally going to ask Riley out?

He almost hyperventilated. He told himself her textspeak and poor punctuation bothered him, but no, it was that she managed to turn the conversation to something he was not ready to talk about.

Though asking Riley Zayat on a real date was definitely on his to do list—and had been for some time—he'd screwed it up royally every time he tried. Strangely, asking Riley out wasn't even making the top ten of today's list of anxieties.

Quickly erasing everything else he'd already started writing before her message had left him frozen, he typed back.

—NO

Christian began typing again, but leave it to Carlisle to be faster than him.

—Why not?

Once again, he erased half of what he'd been typing. Trying to change the direction of the conversation when Carlisle had an idea was like trying to turn the tide. You could run into it, but it would just bowl you over. He ran headfirst into the waves again.

—Jesus, Carlisle. Listen for a second.

He paused for a moment, wondering if yet another text was going to come in from his sister. Or maybe five. But when the moment passed, and nothing pinged his system, Christian hoped maybe she was actually waiting for him.

—I have to be James Bond. Tomorrow.

There was another long pause. Only this one wasn't one that made him think maybe his sister was letting him ask what he wanted. No, this one made him worried. He should have known there was no help for it. The answer had to be "no." Even Carlisle couldn't make that miracle happen. But then his phone bleeped at him again and a tiny cartoon laughing dog rolled across his screen over and over and over. It held its round belly while tears burst out of its eyes.

Sighing, he laid the phone down.

He shouldn't try.

It wasn't worth it. He would do everything he could to help Seven be James Bond Jr. That's what the boy really wanted, right? Though Seven had asked him to play the part of Bond, and though Christian had said *yes* he would just have to say it hadn't worked out.

Ever since the fifth grader said he wanted to grow up and be Q, and that he wanted to be James Bond for his project Christian had taken it upon himself to research the part. So he'd watched three different James Bond movies with three different James Bonds. Each time he picked one up, he'd rejected it as a complete impossibility of achievement.

Not wanting to give up hope, he chose a different movie with a different actor playing the iconic Bond. None had come close to being in his scope. Roger Moore was the closest, and even that Bond was still so far out of his reach that Christian had made the mistake of texting his sister and asking for help.

He was staring out the window, trying to figure out how to break the news to Seven, but his phone pinged him again from where he'd set it face down on the table. He didn't even want to see what it said, but his little sister would raise hell if he didn't answer.

—What's this for?

He waited a moment, not wanting to type back "trying to impress Riley," because that wouldn't go over well. He typed out something more innocuous instead.

—It's a class project.

Though he hoped it wouldn't signal his sister, Christian had no doubt he wasn't anywhere near close to hiding things from her. She read between the lines well enough to read things he didn't know he'd written.

There was another pause. Apparently, it didn't matter what the reason was, clearly making him into James Bond was still patently unachievable.

But when his phone bleeped again it said something different.

—Meet me at the mall. One hour.

He wasn't sure what they were going to do at the mall. He didn't remember anything even remotely like James Bond at their small town eye sore of a mall. But if Carlisle thought she could pull it off, he would trust her.

A moment later, he amended that thought. He didn't trust her, but he would do what she said. She was his best hope. However, she was probably going to tell him he needed to buy a wide variety of things in order to become James Bond. He told himself that women loved James Bond and that Riley would be no exception. Carlisle was his best hope.

As long as she didn't take him to any computer stores to buy laser pointer guns, he would try to play along. At least he had that part taken care of.

He and Seven had been working nonstop to get the toys ready. In fact, Seven had been working at home on various smaller projects. So far, he had turned his YMCA gym membership card into a foldable USB so he could hide it in plain sight. Christian told the boy it was genius, but Seven was most proud that he could still use the card to enter the gym. And that Ever had not yet realized what he'd done.

Together, they'd built a cell phone that also blew up—only it threw out confetti rather than shrapnel. Riley had called him on that one.

"Do you think it's wise to teach that kid the basics of bomb-making?"

Christian had frozen at her question. "I didn't think of it that way. It seemed fun."

She'd nodded at him. Then, just before his heart burst from fear he'd royally fucked up, she smiled. "That's the thing with bright kids. They'll get into things before you even realize it. I don't think Seven is on the road to terrorism. But seriously, don't teach the sixth grade class that stuff!"

Christian had raised an eyebrow at her, but she wouldn't elaborate. He still couldn't figure out which sixth grader she'd been worried about, so he went back to the task at hand of becoming the sexiest man alive.

What a joke. No wonder his sister had sent the laughing dog.

There was no backing out now. Of course, Seven wanted to walk into the room as James Bond Jr. and he wanted Christian with him. So Christian Weaver, who had graduated two years early, and made several million before he graduated college, was about to go make an idiot of himself in the fourth grade.

He gathered his keys, checked his wallet—making sure he had plenty of cash, so he didn't leave a digital trail of embarrassment—and looked in the mirror. He didn't look even close to the part. The only thing he had going for him was a good credit limit so he could spend however many dollars it was going to take to play the fool. With his hopes lower than he thought possible, he headed out the door.

Carlisle met him just inside the food court with a hug and a dubious eye. She looked him up and down before declaring, "We have two jobs today."

"I thought we had one," he protested, then realized the second was probably payment. There must be something that she wanted in return.

"One, we're going to turn you into James Bond. Two, we're going to get you set up to ask Riley Zayat out on a real date."

"I've got the second one taken care of," he told her under his breath.

But again, she looked at him sideways even as she grabbed his hand and dragged him down to one corner of the mall. One of the big stores swallowed them up as she tugged him into the back corner.

When they reached a formal wear section he hadn't even known existed, she waved to the clerk. Then she turned and looked at him. "So how's that going for you?"

"It's fine," he mumbled through gritted teeth. This day was sucking and Carlisle was barely getting started.

"Excellent," Carlisle smiled that Cheshire cat grin at him, "so explain to me then when you're going on this date?"

"Shut up?" He was begging and he knew it. "Carlisle, just help me out."

She narrowed her eyes, but she did stop pestering him about asking his crush out on a date. Then she spent the next several minutes explaining to the clerk that her older brother needed to be James Bond.

While Christian wished he could sink into the floor, the woman in the store measured him as though this was an everyday occurrence. Then she explained how much the tux was going to cost.

Holy shit. He should have rented.

GIFTED

He told Carlisle this but she replied, "No. Look at all us Mayfair cousins. You're going to need this tux."

His mouth fell open and he was grateful for the distraction. Christian was proud of himself, too. Look at him, reading between the lines. "Are you getting married? Is that why I need a tux?"

But, instead of a wide grin or a flash of engagement ring, Carlisle's eyes darted down and to the side. He'd learned to read that long ago. Not liking what he was seeing, he asked "Gary?"

"No Gary. Gary's an ass," she replied.

Well, shit, he thought *another one bit the dust.*

Carlisle was great at beginning relationships. She found wonderful men, had a great time, and fell head over heels in love. Then she invariably found out something horrid about them later. Gary, just now getting the label of "ass" was actually quite a step up from her previous boyfriends. And those were just the ones Christian knew about.

Ward had cheated on her and then lied to her. She'd bought it until she caught him later. That time he'd actually been in the act of cheating on her... and with her good friend. The whole family had said good-riddance to Ward. Jeremy had turned out to be gay. That wasn't a character flaw. He shouldn't have been dating Carlisle, but no, it was the fact that he was manipulative and controlling that was the real problem. Even worse, Axel had hit her.

Christian didn't know how to say that maybe Gary was an improvement. So he just said, "I'm sorry."

They were interrupted by the clerk handing back his credit card and letting him know the tux could be picked up later that night. Christian made the mistake of looking at the bill and almost swallowed his tongue. If he didn't ask Riley out, all this would be a very expensive waste.

Then he told himself, no, Seven wanted it. And the kids would love it. Still...

"Next," Carlisle grabbed him and hauled him off, breaking

through his thoughts. "We need to take care of your hair." His sister said this as though her heart was not broken by Gary The Ass. Maybe it was a good thing that Christian was being a project and maybe it was a good thing that his project was so freaking enormous.

Still, he protested. "I'm not dyeing my hair. I'm not going to be one of those guys."

Carlisle stopped dead in the mall, almost letting him plow into the back of her. She turned and looked up at his hair. "You can't be James Bond with bleached swimmer hair."

"I'm not going to wear a swim cap. I swim almost every morning." He knew there was nothing that could be done about it. At least nothing he was willing to do. Not a cap, not shaving bald, not.. well, in the end, he'd embraced the careless swimmer look.

"Then we have to do something about your hair, James." Carlisle shrugged up at him.

She was right, and he followed along.

❧ 11 ❧

Riley headed down the school hallway, nervous to the point of being frantic.

She'd left the children in the room alone—something she didn't like to do. Something that school policy was generally against. The problem was Christian was late and Seven was starting to get a bit nervous about it.

The boy had showed up today wearing an adorable dark gray suit. It looked fantastic on him, as did his new close-cut hairstyle.

"It's my James Bond Junior hair!" he'd told her. And he'd said Christian was going to show up and play the part of the senior Bond.

But now all the children were getting concerned that Christian was late and so was she. So she skipped her way down the hallway—not a happy skip, but a frantic one—as she headed toward the office, trying to see if Christian had already checked in.

On her way she passed someone she didn't recognize. It was a teacher's job to watch the hallways for strange players in the school. They'd done a teacher inservice day on school safety and everything. So she turned to look at the tall man in a tux as he headed toward her. One hand played with the button on the front of the jacket, the other reached up as if to check his dark hair.

Jesus, if anyone wanted to get into their school this was the way to do it. She tried not to stare right at him, but she wasn't immune. This was a building full of young, mostly female teachers, and this guy... When he smiled at her, she wished she could smile back. But she had to get to the office before anything went wrong in her classroom.

Crap! Who was he and why did he show up now when she was running down the hall? Why couldn't she have the time to at least stop and say hi? To ask if he needed any help and see if he should be allowed in the school? But he passed her, and the moment was gone. At least her kids hadn't blown the school up... yet.

Running a little farther, Riley bumped into Angelia. With a sharp breath, she said, "I just left my kids alone and I'm looking for Christian. Have you seen him?"

"He just went down the hall. You must have missed him—" Angelia started to say something else, but Riley turned on her heels and yelled over her shoulder, "Thank you!"

Almost running back, she prayed nothing had gone wrong. It was poor form to leave any classroom alone, but her kids might paint the room or hack the entire computer system, or... For a moment she was grateful the building was brick.

When Riley arrived at her classroom, she threw open the door to find that the children were all clustered around the tall man in the tux. Only then did she see what she hadn't seen the first time.

Holy crap, that was *Christian*.

He looked up at her and smiled again and this time she wondered why she hadn't recognized it in the hallway—that smile was *his*. She'd always liked it but, good God, it was making her heart thump now.

What in God's name had he done?

Looking him up and down, she noticed the shyness that once again took over his expression. But as he looked down at the kids and answered their questions, she took another moment to check out this new Christian Weaver. His hair no longer had the bleached ends from what she originally thought was the sun, but eventually found out was a daily dose of chlorine.

He'd dyed it brown, back to the natural color that showed at the roots. Combing it back showed off his temples, that jaw line, and the straight nose. It made his gaze more direct. And it made her heart jump into her throat.

The tux showed off the swimmers body that he earned for apparently an hour or so every morning. There was something about swimming that built men up in all the right places and Christian Weaver was no exception. She'd noticed that before, the broad shoulders and casual muscles had shown under the thermal long-sleeved tees. There was an amazing ass under those tux pants, too.

He looked up at her again. "Did you find what you were looking for?"

Her face almost went up in flames before she realized he'd—luckily—not caught her checking him out. He meant when she passed him in the hallway and paid no attention to him because she was looking for *him*.

Rather than explaining the colossal mix up that she'd made, Riley merely said, "Yes, I think I did."

Then she turned to the kids. Finally taking control of the room and her senses, she said, "All right, Seven and Christian —*Mr. Weaver*—" she corrected herself, "have something to show us."

Perching herself in one of the tiny chairs, Riley crossed her legs as she fidgeted. Christian and Seven started their presentation and she quickly realized she needed to be paying more attention to the children in the audience than the man at the front of the room. Still, it was hard to look away.

She'd liked Christian from the start—quite a bit—but she

knew she shouldn't get involved and she hadn't let the feelings go any further. Or maybe she had but she'd been telling herself otherwise. Lord knew her friends had seen right through her even as she'd told them it was nothing.

It wasn't nothing.

James Bond was standing at the front of her classroom and his smile was telling her there was no way to stop what had been thrown into motion.

In case she hadn't tumbled far enough already, Christian stood up with Seven and the two managed to do a whole spy routine for the class. Clearly, this was Seven's doing and not Christian's. Riley knew that Christian would never have headed into the hallway voluntarily, then snuck back in as though he were looking for a hidden gem and pulled out a laser pointer gun.

He and Seven play-acted as though they were stealing information from her computer. For a moment she was grateful the computer did not have her conversations with Bailey Ann and Angelia anywhere on it. What would she do if Christian could read that?

But before her face could flame up too red, Christian asked for a volunteer. "Who wants to be the bad guy?"

When several children volunteered, he and Seven agreed they could take on the lot of them. After all, they were two James Bonds.

In the end, all the kids playing the bad guys faked horrible deaths at the wrong end of Seven's pretend laser gun. Riley was in stitches, as we're the remainder of the kids still in their chairs. Fewer than half were watching; most were participating, with Christian encouraging them to do so.

She'd not expected this of the shy man who'd walked into her room just over a month ago.

She'd not expected James Bond. Or any of this.

When they finished with their sketch, there were still two more hours of class. But Seven had showed up for school today in his suit and had worn it the whole time. As she'd seen coming down the hall, Christian had showed up that way, too. So she was trying to teach her class with Bond, James Bond, hanging out and doing a damn good job of distracting her.

Riley found it tough to keep her concentration where it needed to be, so she hyper focused on the children who still needed help with their projects. Christian had another task for the rest of the afternoon, and he enlisted Seven to help with some of the other kids. "It's good to be a helper sometimes and not the leader."

Seven was proud to be in the "teacher" role for once and started walking around seeing who needed him. Because she'd thrown herself into her work helping Jacob and Liam, Riley didn't notice right away what had happened.

Screeches came from the other side of the room and—as was usual in her teacher persona—she remained outwardly calm, but immediately jumped to help. Lisa Lynn looked about one second away from putting her fist through the computer screen. In her other hand she clutched a cell phone tight enough to crush it had her hands been any bigger.

When she waved it back and forth while she yelled, Christian slid up behind her and Riley watched. How would he handle this? A month ago, he would have shied away from a child nearing a meltdown. He still didn't seem to take to it too well, but he had better coping mechanisms himself.

Hanging back, Riley watched as he flinched at the shrill voice but leaned over the tiny desk. Hovering over the little girl, he gently took the phone out of her grip. After setting it down he turned the little chair around and took both her hands. Getting the little girl to look at him, he asked what was wrong. It was a play right out of Riley's own book. He had to have been watching her do that with the kids when they got worked up.

Lisa Lynn sucked in a breath and wailed. "It won't work! It works on the computer, but it won't work on my phone. It's supposed to work on my phone. That's how we wrote it!"

Christian started to explain where the coding error had come from, but Lisa Lynn was having none of it. She was too far gone, already melted down into tears and sniffles. As Riley watched, Christian calmly seated himself in the chair next to the little girl, even though it was—as always—far too small for him.

He stroked Lisa Lynn's hair and let her cry and, when her irritation got a little too big for her, she crawled into his lap. He held on to her. Whatever he was saying to the girl, Riley couldn't hear, but it was working. In a moment, the little girl looked up and said, "So if I check the code for errors one more time and I don't find anything, you'll help me?"

"Yes," he said, still calm despite Lisa Lynn's red face and tears. "Should we check it together?"

Riley knew right then she was in far more trouble than she'd imagined.

❧ 12 ❦

Riley sat in her big comfy chair with her feet tucked up under her. She was wearing her softest leggings and her big sweatshirt, hoping to be comfortable while she talked with her friend on the phone. However, the conversation was anything but.

"I saw him," Angelia said, "And I saw the way you looked at him even before he turned up at the school in a damn tux."

It was a hard truth that Riley was admitting to herself. She knew she liked Christian, knew she enjoyed working with him. She also knew she was attracted to him. But she'd managed to keep telling herself *No*. She would simply admire him from the other side of her classroom, but she wouldn't get involved.

He was one of her volunteers and the children had to be her first priority. She told Angelia exactly that, "I came here as soon as I graduated my master's program with my certificate in hand. I moved to Breathless just to get this job."

"I know," her friend replied. But Riley wasn't certain that her friend truly understood.

"I came across the country to find a town that would fund a gifted class. Then I taught third grade for two years, waiting for the old gifted teacher to retire. And you know I worked my ass off to get into position to take this class myself."

"What are you *really* saying?" Angelia asked her.

No, this conversation was not going to get more comfortable. *Crap*. Riley squirmed. She didn't want her friend thinking that teaching third grade was a step down. That's not what she'd meant. Angelia taught third and Riley may have just put her foot in it. She tried to explain her way out of it. "I'm saying I can't give up this job over a man—a man who might not even be attracted to me in return!"

Luckily, Angelia seemed to take no insult at Riley's inadvertent jab. But she did turn the conversation back. "So what's your worst case scenario?"

Riley knew she probably wasn't going to come out of this with any secrets intact. But, God forbid, she did have a scenario that—if Angelia agreed with her—would mean Riley needed to back off somehow. If her job could really be put in jeopardy, then she couldn't risk it. "What if I get fired?"

"That would mean," Angelia started again, "that Christian Weaver filed a sexual harassment suit against you and *won* it." She paused, then added with a sly tone, "Have you been harassing him in class Riley?"

At least Riley could laugh at that. "No, I have not been sexually harassing my volunteers."

"Then, you don't have to worry about getting fired," her friend told her. "Probably your real worst case scenario is that he leaves you holding the bag with those kids. That you wind up with projects you can't help with and Christian won't come back to class. That would hurt the kids, probably a lot."

Angelia understood what it was to be dedicated to her classroom. Riley had fought hard to get a lot of them admitted to her program. She pushed the parents to test them, pushed them to sign the paperwork. She'd even fought a few cases where the parents insisted the child *wasn't* gifted, just a troublemaker. Riley had scores that proved otherwise. Her heart and soul was in this job.

"What's the likelihood of that actually happening? Of Christian leaving you hanging because you asked him out?"

That gave Riley pause, but she knew the answer. "It's very low. Christian won't bail on the kids, though if he gets uncomfortable, he might not want to return or spend time around me."

"Look, if you make him that uncomfortable, then this is a problem," Angelia agreed for the first time. "Have you tried anything to feel it out?"

Riley thought for a moment, "I asked him to coffee the first week."

"How did that go?"

Oh, Riley thought. *It went well. Just no dating.* "We go every week."

"Do you now?" Angelia pushed her tone.

"Maybe he'll ask me out. I mean, we go to coffee and he could ask me out any time. Then the whole situation would be fine."

"But you go to coffee every week and he hasn't asked yet."

Crap. She was right. But Angelia continued. "I hate to break this to you, but he's not going to ask you out. In the brief time I've been around him, I figured that much out. He's as concerned—or maybe *more concerned* than you are—about the classroom dynamic. He's an impressive man, but he's not a player." Angelia paused. "I think he wants to go out with you, but by the time he makes a move, you'll have moved to another city."

Riley could pretty much agree with that assessment.

If a move was going to be made, it would have to be hers.

Still her friend pushed. "Doesn't his mother also work in your classroom? Westerley Weaver is not going to let him file sexual harassment charges against you! Not over asking him out. Besides, he's going to say yes. I'm confident you're safe. Just ask once and see what happens."

Angelia was right. Ask once. No would mean no.

Riley turned to face the other direction. She dangled her legs over the side of her armchair and leaned her back against the pillow. "You're right. I'm going to have to screw up the courage to do this. I don't think I've ever asked a man out before!"

Angelia should have ignored that, but she didn't. "Equality is equality. So, what inspired this today? Was it that tux? Because the tux was hot, but why was he wearing a tux to an elementary school?"

Riley explained about Christian and Seven and James Bond. She told about how he'd handled Lisa Lynn's meltdown at the computer when her program wouldn't transfer to her phone app. She could practically hear Angelia fanning herself from the other side of the phone.

"Oh girl, you are in trouble. He melted your panties. And then he melted your heart."

"Pretty much," Riley replied.

"Well, look, if you're not going to ask him out, please step aside so I can."

"He's not your type!" Riley protested.

"Yeah I thought you'd say that." The lilt of Angelia's retort let Riley know she'd walked neatly into that trap.

They talked for a few more minutes about how Riley should go about asking Christian on a date. They discussed her best options, then Riley hung up the phone and paced her way around her small living room for a while. She tried to figure out how to make herself do this. It was hard, getting up the nerve to ask someone out.

She wondered if he'd still have that dark James Bond hair tomorrow. She wondered how she would look at him, now that she'd seen this side of him. Now that she knew there was a James-Bond-worthy bod under those thermal T's and nice slacks.

Shit. She was in so deep.

She poured a glass of wine and told herself tomorrow was Friday, a good day for her little endeavor. She could ask him out, and if he said no, then they'd have four days to recover before they had to see each other again. It was ideal. Except for the part where it took so much guts.

Riley finished the wine and put the glass in the sink, even though her nerves told her to fill it back up. When she finally went to sleep that night, she had vivid dreams of Christian Weaver.

✥ 13 ✥

"**N**o, that's not where that goes." Riley tried to keep the snap out of her voice as she helped Robert put away the pieces of his project.

Each kid had his or her own space on the shelf. She'd not seen a need to label the spots with tape and names, she was thinking these kids were bright enough to remember where their things went. Mostly, it worked, though Robert kept trying to put his in the wrong place. Today that bothered her.

"Are you okay, Miss Zayat?" the little boy asked, looking up at her, his bag of supplies still clutched in his hands. At least he looked confused and not scared.

"I think she's just got something on her mind." Christian's voice came from over her shoulder, not knowing how right he was.

Riley was as nervous as if she were going on stage. She'd never asked anyone out before, and now she was wondering how men did it all the time. She believed in equality; she just hadn't been quite prepared for it.

"I'm fine," she told both of them with as much smile as she could genuinely muster, then she turned back to the boy. "Robert, you need to keep your things in the proper place on the shelf. If you don't, they'll be in one of the other kid's spots. Then somebody else will use your materials, and you won't have your supplies."

Robert nodded, seeming to understand, though she had no idea if he'd remember it next week. She watched as he put his things into his designated space, but she wasn't fine. She was wound up and Christian kept staring at her chest.

Did he know what she was planning? She had no idea if she was being obvious or just cranky.

This week had been a bit off from their schedule. They'd gone out to coffee on Wednesday instead of Thursday, because Christian had an appointment. It turned out he wasn't as rigidly structured as she'd originally thought. And his sense of humor— while it took a moment to uncover—was sharp and wicked, exactly as Riley liked it.

She felt a tug at the side of her skirt and looked down.

"Miss Zayat, it's time for us to go back to our classrooms." Leigh was looking up at her with those big eyes and her usual concern that things might get out of order.

Angry with herself for missing the time, Riley's eyes darted up to the clock. Yes, they were late. "You're right!"

She clapped her hands in the way she always did to get the children's attention and lined them up at the door. In a moment, they were all gone down the hallway, and the classroom had too quickly changed from a bustling cove of activity to an empty box just waiting for her to make her move.

She'd been telling herself all day that she could do this. Her little mental pep talks worked at the time, but now that the time was here, she turned to Christian and opened her mouth like a fish. He was still staring at her chest, and she had no idea what to say.

"Your blouse has code on it," he said, pointing at her breasts and Riley almost dissolved into laughter.

Christian was not so crass as to be staring at someone's chest, certainly not in front of children. No, he was trying to read her shirt. She probably shouldn't have worn a shirt people would have to decipher. She'd just thought of it as a neat design from one of her favorite stores for teacher wear.

She pulled the bottom of it out, to flatten the design so he didn't have to read it over her breasts. She confessed, "Does it mean anything in particular? I don't know."

He shook his head. "I've been trying to read it all afternoon. And I just realized it looks like I've been staring at your boobs. And I wasn't... Well, I was, but I didn't mean to be."

Though she felt bad about his obvious concern that he'd been staring at her chest, she still wanted to laugh. This was becoming as awkward as it possibly could be. But at least with the code shirt, they had something to talk about.

"It doesn't code for anything in particular," he eventually said once he realized she wasn't angry. "There are a few lines that make sense, but all together—" He waved his hand up and down her front, "I don't think it would make anything useful."

She laughed again, grateful for the explanation of his strange behavior all day. She could only hope her next question would explain hers. But Christian once again filled the space, proving he was far more flexible than she had originally given him credit for. "Your dress yesterday had weird little animals on it."

"Ah, yes." She smiled. "Tardigrades."

"What's a tardigrade?"

"They're small, microscopic multi legged animals."

Christian stared at her as if he was wondering if that was a real thing.

So she said "Yes, they are real." And in that moment while her mouth was already moving and words were already coming out, she just put it out there. "Would you like to go out to dinner with me?"

Of course, as soon as she said it, it became clear that she had been *unclear*. They went out to coffee all the time—as friends, as a thank you for his volunteer work. Dinner could easily be misunderstood as more of the same. Lord knew, he'd done enough work to merit a full meal.

He nodded in response, but it wasn't quite enough. She knew if she went out for an evening meal with Christian and didn't make it obvious that this was a date, it probably wouldn't be one. So Riley tried again, "I'm asking you out. I was thinking maybe you'd like to go to the new Italian place over on Broadway?"

She let the question hang, but he stared at her as though he were thinking.

Well shit, she thought. She didn't want him to have to think about it. She'd hoped he was as interested as she was.

But then he said, "No."

Double shit, she thought as her heart sank and she felt her forced-wide smile start to falter. Then she consoled herself with her earlier mantra: at least she'd gained the experience. She could now say she had made the effort and asked someone out. Now she knew what that kind of rejection felt like.

Go, team Riley! She was sarcastic even in her thoughts.

She'd promised herself she would only ask once. No meant no. So she nodded at him and turned away, trying to hide her disappointment, the depth of which she hadn't been fully prepared for.

"Have you been to that restaurant?" Christian asked her back, the only part she was showing him as she tried to get herself together.

Riley found she was disappointed at his question. She'd hoped he would say his "No" and leave her alone to wallow in it. She didn't turn around though. "No, I haven't. I've heard the food is very good though."

"It is, but the place is noisy. It would be nicer if we could eat somewhere quieter." Then he paused. "Somewhere we could talk." He paused again. "If this is going to be a date."

Hope flared in her chest, and she was shocked at the roller coaster. She expected this to be easier—not easy, but easier than *this*. Yes, no, no, yes. But she was on yes, and she was going to take it.

She turned, knowing she wasn't able to keep the smile off her face or the light from her eyes. Christian Weaver had just said *yes*. She'd make it work. "So how about I go pick up dinner and I meet you..."

She trailed off, not knowing if it was appropriate to invite him to her place. Or was it right to go to his?

"You can come to my house," he volunteered quickly, as though he wanted to make this work out as much as she did. "I can pick up the food."

"No," she replied, putting her foot down, confident at least in this. She smiled as she said it; she might not have been able to *not* smile. "I asked you out, I'm paying for dinner. Just tell me what you want, and I'll pick it up and bring it to your place."

She could trust him. There was nothing about Christian Weaver that made her concerned. She knew she shouldn't go to a man's place on a first date, but this was Christian. Riley found she trusted him implicitly, and that was almost as wonderful a feeling as him saying yes.

She suggested six and waited while he checked his watch then said, "I think I'll need until seven to get ready."

That piqued her interest. She was going to have to ask him what needed the time. But a few moments later Christian said, "thank you," and left it at that before he was out the door.

Riley was finally alone in the classroom. She looked around the space, looked out the window, checked to see if anyone was walking by in the hallway. She was grateful today that she was on one of the upper floors and no one could see her. Then she jumped up and down in the middle of her classroom and squealed with delight.

Christian Weaver had said yes.

❧ 14 ❧

Christian felt his nerves kick up. He'd been on dates before, but mostly when he'd asked out women that he liked. When they said yes, he dated them... until things fell apart.

He knew he was smart; he knew he was weird; he knew his parents were big names around town and that he had more than the average amount of money in his bank account. He'd tried to hide all of that in the past. Needless to say, it had never worked out. Even when it seemed to, eventually he was too weird or not interested in what she was doing or something, and it would be over.

Nothing like Riley Zayat had ever happened to him before.

And he was not prepared.

His house was only partially furnished. When he lived in California, his home had been much smaller and much more expensive. So he'd arrived in Breathless without much more than a comfy couch and a big TV. He had a big bed and small dresser and one very nice set of barstools that he put at the kitchen breakfast counter when he set the place up. But when Riley asked him out and suggested bringing dinner, he realized he didn't even have a table. Or chairs.

He'd left her there in the classroom, maybe a little too rapidly and without explanation, but he'd needed *furniture*. He screwed the last bolt into the underside of the table, as the store had insisted it travel in two pieces. They'd offered to deliver and assemble it—tomorrow. So Christian had taken it on himself, attaching the center stand while he worried that it was getting too close to seven p.m. and Riley was going to catch him building his home.

He'd hauled the big box in the door, unpacked all the pieces and then climbed into the shower. He couldn't shower after she got here, but—if he had to—he could assemble the table. The chairs came ready to go. He'd picked out nicer ones with padded seats and backs. It was a faster move than he liked—he preferred to think about his decisions—and he wasn't a fan of wooden chairs. But Riley Zayat was coming for a date, and the table had suddenly become required.

With the furniture in his car, he'd figured he should get a tablecloth, too. While he was at the bed and bath store, he saw the dinnerware section and realized his silverware was also lacking. Certainly a southern woman like Riley wouldn't appreciate the cheap, stamped pieces that he'd bought at a Restaurant Supply for a song.

He grabbed a box of well-weighted Oneida at the store, and while he was picking out the tablecloth, he discovered the adjacent display of matching cloth napkins. He grabbed a batch in a blue he liked and thought it would be appropriate for this evening.

As he walked around the store collecting item after item that he suddenly, desperately needed, his basket got heavier and heavier. He should have used a cart. He shouldn't have started this craziness. But he thought about Riley bringing a nice dinner and the two of them eating side by side at his breakfast counter and added a set of four placemats into the basket. God help him, he was becoming his mother.

He'd put the silverware into the drawer after washing and drying it. But he left the fabric items out while he twisted the last screw in tightly and tested everything. God forbid their dishes slide off the table in the middle of the meal.

His phone buzzed just then, and he looked over to see a message from Riley. His heart thumped, suddenly afraid she was canceling. There was no reason for her to do so, but it remained a concerning possibility until he read the message.

—Sorry, food took a little longer than planned, running about five minutes late.

Good, he thought. *Five extra minutes*. He could use them. He grabbed the table and flipped it upright before texting back.

—No worries.

The five minutes would do him good. He'd really pushed on what he could accomplish before she arrived. He'd followed the bed and bath store with a whim—a trip to the liquor store. While there he bought far more than they could drink in one night. Not knowing what she liked, he bought juices, beer, hard cider, and a bottle each of red and white wine.

He knew nothing about most of it, and had asked his way around, listening intently, as the clerk told him, "This red is mid-level. Not too dry, not too sweet. It's a safe bet if you don't know what they prefer."

Christian had nodded but the man asked, "What are you eating for dinner?"

"Italian," he said, which was all he knew. He did understand that white was more for fish and red for steak, but he had no idea what she was bringing.

Riley had asked, "What do you like? What do you want me to order?" She'd been smart enough to tack on. "Is there anything you won't eat?"

It had been embarrassing to give her his list. He was a grown man, but rather than suffer a dinner he wouldn't eat, he told her, "No squash, zucchini, eggplant, or mushrooms."

He'd watched her face, but she just nodded. She was polite about it, but he took a moment to wonder if he'd ruined the date before it even started. He was going to try to not mess it up with a poor wine choice.

Luckily, the clerk was smiling. "What you want is a Chianti! It goes with everything Italian."

Through his relief, Christian proceeded to take more advice and buy the most expensive chianti they had. He added a bottle of Chardonnay, wondering if it was possible to go wrong with something so simple. Then he thought that if it was possible, he could probably manage it.

At home, he'd even considered putting his tux back on. At least that was something he knew she liked, but instead, he put on a button-down shirt and a pair of comfortable pants. The tux was overkill, he knew. He wanted to look nice. He wanted Riley to be attracted to him the way he was to her, but his mother had once told him an uncomfortable man was never attractive.

So he did what he could. She would either still be attracted to him at the end of the evening, or she wouldn't. It felt totally out of his control. So, he laid out the tablecloth—a thing he should be able to control—and frowned at the wrinkles. Ten minutes later, he'd gotten it steamed a little, but it was as good as he could get it without paying a dry-cleaner.

He was setting out his plain white plates when somehow, over the sound of his own breathing, he heard a car outside. For the fourth time, he pulled back the curtain and looked, but this time it was really her. His heartbeat kicked up another notch and he headed for the front door.

Stepping down the front walk, he met her and wondered if his face showed everything he was feeling. "Can I help with the bags?"

She had one in each hand and was honestly doing fine. But he needed something to do and was grateful when she handed one over. It was heavier than he expected. "How much food did you buy?"

"Hmm, probably way too much." She smiled like she had a secret and followed him up the walk.

Opening the door, he pushed inside and turned the corner to put the bags on the kitchen counter. "You changed your clothes."

"So did you," she pointed out with a cute grin. "I couldn't have you trying to read my chest all night."

Oh, dear God, he thought as his hands stopped their motion from laying out the food. "I'm so sorry! I didn't mean—"

Her hand popped up and her smile got wider as she waved him off, allowing him to relax again.

"I was kidding. I just wanted to look nice."

"Me, too." He added the two words before he thought better of it then returned to unpacking the food. The silence settled in between them a little awkwardly, but it only lasted a moment. This was Riley, and one of her great talents, it seemed, was putting him at ease.

"I got us a chicken dish, a fish dish and a pasta."

He turned and stared at her. "Is someone else joining us?"

"No," she laughed. "I was just indecisive. And I didn't know if the portions were small."

"Okay," he decided to take her comment at face value—he'd always been able to trust what she said. But he hefted one of the heavy containers at her and she shrugged.

"Okay, I overshot. Oh, and I got dessert."

"Three?"

"No! I managed to hold back and only get two desserts." But she was smiling again, and it felt right.

"I got wine," he offered and enjoyed the surprise on her face. "Don't look at me that way. I know nothing about wine. I got what the clerk recommended. It's a chianti."

"Then that's what we'll drink!" She took the straw-wrapped bottle from where he held it up and opened his cupboard to search for glasses.

He looked up, realizing he'd failed at becoming his mother. His mother was always prepared. His sister had inherited that.

His younger brother Charlie, Carlisle's twin, had managed to live a life where it didn't matter. No one went to Charlie's for dinner and wine. Charlie was climbing a rock face and photographing a bird or jumping out of an airplane.

But Christian was standing here, staring at his half empty cupboard that didn't have any wine glasses. He felt Riley beside him as she reached up, brushing against him and pulling two glasses down. "These will do."

It felt better to open the drawer and see all the shiny new silverware. Together they plated up the still-steaming food and put everything out on the table. At least the silver tablecloth that he'd picked showed off the plain white dishes. He hadn't thought to get new plates.

Riley didn't seem to notice, though. But she smiled at the tablecloth and cloth napkins.

"What no candles?" she asked

Christian felt his heart stutter. "I—"

"Stop, Christian," she told him again, one hand up warding him off. "I'm having a great time. And I will quit teasing you. You pulled out all the stops."

"I bought the table," he conceded.

She frowned. "Tonight?"

He nodded and tried the Chianti, wondering if a little alcohol wouldn't calm his nerves. For all his missteps, she was still here, still smiling. He pointed toward the breakfast bar. "That was the only option. If you hadn't been a few minutes late, you could have watched me put it together."

"Well, then, here's to the maiden voyage of the new table." She held her glass up until he clinked it. "And don't worry, I don't need candlelight. I'm a bit of a klutz and I would feel really bad if I burned your house down."

He laughed this time, thankful that she was just Riley.

But it was only a moment before she said, "This dish comes with mushrooms, but I had them leave it off. No squash, no mushrooms, no zucchini, no eggplant for you. No peppers or peas for me."

He felt his heart settle squarely into his chest.

She knew what she was doing, she was making him more comfortable and doing an amazing job of it. Now, he just had to figure out where the evening was going.

❧ 15 ❧

Riley had made it all the way through Monday's school day still floating on a bit of a cloud after Friday's date. Unlike Friday, when she'd been nervous and snappy, today she'd been serene... and probably just as absent minded!

The children had left the classroom to go back to their homerooms and she had the place to herself, except for her volunteers. She turned to straighten shelves the second graders had laid waste to, but it didn't surprise her when Westerley Weaver's voice came from over her shoulder. "So I hear you and Christian went out last Friday..."

Riley turned and faced the older woman. "Yes, ma'am, we did."

There was no point in denying it. Clearly, Christian had told her. Or word had gotten around. Riley had gone to a popular restaurant and ordered food for two. Anyone could have seen her coming or going from his place. It was a small town. She was an elementary school teacher. He was the golden boy. Riley was still trying to figure out what had gotten them caught when another voice came into the conversation.

"Oh, what is this?" Bailey Anne suddenly perked up from the other side of the room. "Christian asked you out?"

This. This was that moment where she got to explain herself. So maybe Christian hadn't told his mother everything. Maybe he hadn't told her at all. "Actually, I asked him."

Riley was not prepared for Bailey Ann, sweet Southern belle that she was, to saunter across the room and high five her with a sportsmanlike "Yes!" But that's exactly what her friend did.

However, as soon as the high five was completed Bailey Ann turned, a serious expression on her face. "Are you going out again?"

Riley was cautious. As much as she liked both of these women, they were Christian's family. She didn't want to come between him and them. And she didn't want them to come between her and him, but there was no point in lying. "Yes, there's a band he likes playing in Alpharetta on Tuesday night."

His mother only nodded, and Riley wasn't quite sure how to interpret it. But it only took a moment for Mrs. Weaver to clear things up. "Well, just so you know, I'm going to stay out of this. Christian is his own self and I'm your classroom volunteer."

There was a small smirk on her lips, though, as if maybe she had planned for this to happen. Normally, Riley would have been upset if one of her classroom volunteers was trying to set her up. Since they were setting her up with Christian Weaver it was hard to complain.

Bailey looked between the two of them, her expression serious, her hands on her hips. "I'm not sure *I'll* make any such promise, but I will refrain from chatting about it while his mama is in the room."

"Well, I think you make a good match," Mrs. Weaver volunteered as she tried to turn the toy robots off but kept making them make noise or start to dance. Riley would have helped but instead she thought, *so much for not talking about it.*

Even as she thought the words, it was Bailey Ann who jumped to her rescue. For such a prim Southern belle, that girl always had her back. "Westerley! I thought you just said—"

Westerley stopped her niece and got Riley's attention with a well-placed hand cutting through the air. "I said I wouldn't talk about the two of them dating. I did not say I would not talk up my boy."

It was a fine distinction and Riley could see it even if she didn't quite agree that it held. Still, she wasn't going to tell Westerley Weaver "no." The woman was a powerhouse.

This time Westerley spoke directly to Bailey Ann. Probably another loophole that she thought was perfectly legit. "I think they're good for each other."

When she turned back to Riley. She said, "I wish he would have had a teacher like you, when he was a kid... It's something I've been meaning to say for a while and part of the reason I got into volunteering for this program." She finally got the robot turned off and put away, but she wasn't done talking.

"I didn't know what to do with him when he was little. He started speaking very early, and then he kind of refused to talk to us for a while. We thought something was wrong with his development. Later, he would utter whole sentences with vocabulary we had no idea he knew!"

"I'm sure they were grammatically correct," Bailey Ann threw in from the other side of the room where she was shutting down the computers. Riley raised her eyebrows. Her friend probably wasn't wrong.

She didn't want to ask questions, but she was listening. This was interesting information. Even so, it didn't surprise her. It didn't surprise her either when Westerley Weaver continued telling about her baby boy.

"He was reading by the age of three. And we caught him on his daddy's computer one night just hitting keys."

"Please, God. Tell me, he didn't find the porn!" Bailey Ann said.

Riley wasn't sure if Bailey Ann was really like this—the one to jump into conversation with a quip—or if she was just trying to save Riley's butt from an embarrassing conversation. Bailey Ann was just that well versed in the art of being a good Southern belle that she might be trying to stop her aunt before she said something in front of her son's new date.

Westerley didn't quite get the hint.

"No, it wasn't porn. He was looking at animals on Britannica." She looked around the room for her next task and kept talking. "We put him in kindergarten as soon as they would let us, but he was already way ahead. So we skipped him a grade, thinking it would get him the right level of education." Her southern accent bled through all the words, as did her heart. "I had a template for my whole life," Westerley Weaver told the girls, "I knew how everything was going to go, until Christian came along.

"He hit some of his milestones early and some late. He baffled his doctors with how bright he was, and we didn't know what to do with him. You know, Charlie and Carlisle came along and they did everything according to plan. They were easy." But now she looked Riley in the eyes and Riley felt the intensity of it. "I don't think I always did right by him."

"What do you mean?" Riley asked. "He loves you. You're a great mom."

"I'm glad for that, because I messed up plenty. I tried so hard to make him be normal. And you know what he was never meant for normal. He was always meant for bigger things and I think I held him back."

That was something Riley understood all too well. There were plenty of kids in her classroom whose parents were trying to fit them into some kind of preconceived mold. Carter's dad wanted him to be a baseball player and Carter enjoyed it plenty, but it wasn't what he loved. She wasn't sure what Jacob's parents would think of his project being clothing and sewing based, but she wasn't going to be the one to hold the talented boy back.

"You did a good job," she told Westerley. Parents needed to hear that, she knew. Her volunteer didn't reply and the conversation and the room tidying came to a close. Riley wasn't sure yet if all the things Mrs. Weaver had laid at her feet were things she needed to know about Christian, but they'd been interesting and it was hard to turn down good intel.

Then, when Westerley and Bailey headed out the door, Riley was left alone in the classroom. She still had papers to grade and plans to make and turn in, but all she could do was sit at her desk and relive that kiss.

They'd talked all through dinner, and she'd finally decided nothing was going to happen. There she'd gone and gotten all excited that Christian Weaver had said yes, and then... she helped him put the dishes in the sink and clean up.

She'd even done the lame, "I had a good time." But to a guy like Christian it probably wasn't read as the signal she'd intended it to be.

Riley had been reaching for her coat with one hand, trying to keep the disappointment off her face when she'd felt his fingers brush the back of her other hand.

"Riley?"

She'd turned to face him. But her expectation hadn't mattered. He'd been closer than she knew. She'd felt her mouth fall open and her breath gasp in. She smelled him, and he smelled good, and her nerves tripped.

His voice was low, almost as though they were sharing a secret. "Before you go... is this okay?"

Her voice was gone, stolen by the hitch in her breath, the feel of him moving the air around her. She was stunned by how much she suddenly wanted him. So she nodded.

Christian moved slowly, allowing her to back out, to change her mind, but God, she didn't want to. She didn't know how long it took before his mouth brushed hers, but when it did, the rest of the world disappeared.

The kiss was soft, but not tentative. He wasn't asking. He'd already asked and she'd said yes. She lifted onto her toes, pressing them together as his hands came up her back. She felt his chest move as he breathed, as his hands roved up her spine, caressing more than holding. Christian would never cage her in.

He didn't need to. His touch was a gravitational force she couldn't escape.

His mouth parted against hers, his tongue seeking, and Riley was willingly found. Her arms looped around his waist, the button-down shirt hiding nothing of the hard feel of him against her. She pushed up higher on her toes, her whole body molding against him as she did. He made a noise in response and she wanted to, too. But she tightened her arms around him and kissed him back.

Eventually, he'd stepped back, his arms going loose around her. She was breathing heavily and could see that he was, too. It was good to know that he wasn't immune to whatever drug-like high was between them.

His voice still sounded like a whisper, full of change and promise. "I should stop before that goes too far, but I've wanted to do that for a long time."

"Me, too," she'd whispered back, still looking up at him. But she'd grabbed her coat and gone out the door without another word.

Riley blinked into the empty classroom. Thank God no one was here to see her. Her face was probably flushed and she had no idea if she'd been making expressions that told anyone watching exactly what she thought of Christian Weaver's hot mouth.

She had to get her shit together. This was not the first time she'd relived that kiss since Friday night. And it likely wouldn't be the last...

❧ 16 ❧

Say what you want about the South, but no one retires and moves up north.

CHRISTIAN STOOD ON RILEY'S DOORSTEP, A BOUQUET OF flowers in one hand, a bag of rich smelling food in the other, and a grin on his face.

He left the classroom a little early today, letting Riley and the kids know that he had a meeting to get to. He'd thought he was playing it cool, but clearly he had no concept of that. Because Seven had caught on that something was between them.

He'd tapped Christian on the arm, "Mr. Weaver." He paused slightly as though framing his words, then he asked, "Are you going out with Miss Zayat?"

Christian hadn't known how to answer that. And he'd frozen for a moment before looking up and across the room. As always, Riley seemed to know everything that was going on. Though she was working with several other kids in a different group, she lifted her head and smiled at Seven's comment. So Christian told the boy, "Yes"

He'd mistakenly thought that would be the end of it, but no.

Seven tapped him on the arm again and asked, "Are you Miss Zayat's boyfriend?"

It wasn't something they'd discussed. Were they exclusive? Were they going to tell people? His mother and sister had gotten it out of him, but he'd held back as much as possible, letting go of only the barest details. And in the middle of a classroom was not the time or the place for that discussion. Floundering, Christian again looked up and across the room and Riley gave him a very subtle nod.

Interesting, he thought. Date number three was tonight, but she was willing to call him her boyfriend now. He looked down at the boy with a renewed appreciation for overly personal questions. "Yes," he told Seven.

Of course, Seven followed that up with, "Is Miss Zayat your girlfriend?" as though that would work any other way. Christian couldn't figure that out. But again he smiled and said yes. The goofy grin on his face must have grown, because as soon as he answered that third question, it set Seven free with some magical power. The young boy turned to the whole room and practically yelled, "Mr. Weaver and Miss Zayat are boyfriend and girlfriend!"

That had sent the whole room off into a fit of giggles, but Christian had liked the smile on Riley's face. He would have kissed her before he left the room. But the children were there and he had to leave. It would have been inappropriate, but damn, it would have been great.

The band Tuesday Night had been wonderful. But as he had suspected, the place was noisy, and while they enjoyed it, they hadn't gotten to talk much. He was looking forward to being at her place tonight.

He liked it when it was just the two of them together and he wondered where it might lead. It seemed pretty intense by the numbers. They'd gone out Tuesday and now Thursday. He knew the intensity of his feelings, but he wasn't sure that was a good measure. Riley Zayat had quickly become his dream girl, so dating her in the real world was throwing him for all kinds of loops.

He was wondering what she thought of this dating schedule, because Riley had to get up in the morning and go to school. It sounded weird, a grown woman having to go to school, but he didn't have to even be at work. He could sleep in. But it was literally a school night for Riley. He would try to keep that in mind as the evening wore on.

This time he was bringing dinner—Mexican food from a hole on the wall he'd found on the other side of town. If they kept eating like this, he was going to have to swim extra laps each morning to make up for it.

She opened the door just as he was looking around the front of her small home. She lived in a townhouse condo in a long chain of units. A little bit of German trim livened up the light colors and the brick. From the front door, he could see a straight shot past her kitchen on the left and stairs on the right, straight through the living area to the large windows and sliding glass door at the back. They led to a pretty patio enclosed by a tall wood fence. There was a metal table and matching chairs, some plants that would likely bloom in various colors in the spring.

He liked it. It was pretty and the whole place looked like Riley. Not like his house. Hers was *lived in*. She probably didn't have to assemble a table so he could come over, and he liked the idea of the patio, but it was too cold outside. He wouldn't get to take advantage of the pretty space outside for a while, probably.

He wondered if he'd still be around in the spring to enjoy the patio. If they'd still be together. But he told himself not to think that far ahead.

She was pulling the flowers out of his fist. "These are beautiful. Thank you. Can I help carry anything else?"

But Christian shook his head and transferred the bags before following her into her kitchen this time.

"Look what I got!" she told him, opening the fridge and

revealing Margarita mix and hard ciders in several varieties. "I thought we'd try them out."

He'd confessed Tuesday night at the concert that he didn't like beer. She'd laughed at him for buying it the week before.

"But maybe *you* liked it," he'd protested. Now, the little things were falling in line. Even three dates in, he knew to get her food without bell peppers. She knew that buying him beer was a waste of money. He knew how she tasted…

"This seemed to go with Mexican food," she told him, bringing his thoughts back into reality. "And I haven't tried any of these brands. So I have no idea if they're any good or not. Which one do you want to start with?"

She asked it as he was opening up styrofoam containers. Not quite as classy as what she'd brought over, but he'd had it before and he knew it was good. He picked a bottle and she split it between two glasses, handing his half over to taste.

"That's pretty good," he said, tasting it and liking the tart flavor. But then he set the glass on the counter and reached out. He'd been waiting since Tuesday to touch her again. "I missed you."

She grinned up at him. "You saw me yesterday and today."

"Yeah, but I couldn't do this." With his arm around her waist he gently tugged at her. He wouldn't force; it was always better when he knew she wanted him as much as he wanted her. He felt her fingers curl into the front of his shirt, felt the tug at the fabric as she pulled him down and her up. Their lips met in a wash of heat and feeling.

She fit. She felt perfect. She pushed against him, letting him feel her form riding up against his. He breathed her in, kissed her back. He loved the feel of her ass under his hand, her hair in the other. He loved the way she moved against him. The way she always seemed to be seeking an even closer connection between them.

He was holding her tight against him when he felt her head pull back. His arms loosened, and the fists she tugged at his shirt with now pushed a little against him. She stepped back. *Had he over stepped?*

"We're not going to get dinner if we keep doing that." She was breathing heavily, but there was a light in her eyes. She wasn't mad, but he took it for a signal.

Either she was hungry. Or she wanted to continue, but he was moving too fast.

So he nodded and picked up both the plates, letting her follow along. He laid the plates out at the table as she set down the glasses and the bottle of hard cider. And he tried to get his breathing under control.

They talked easily through the meal, and the tight chest that he often felt when he was on dates loosened every time he was around her. It was a comfortable feeling, and he'd wondered at times if he liked her because she made him comfortable. But that wasn't it.

Still, he had a moment's apprehension and he looked up, pausing in the middle of the meal. "Why do you like me, Riley?"

She blinked, as clearly he'd caught her off guard, and he almost apologized. But he wanted to know. If she didn't actually want *him*, then he needed to get out before he got in way too deep. So he changed the subject just for a moment, because maybe this was the better thing to ask, an easier answer. "Are you attracted to me? Because I am attracted to you. Very much so."

That, at least, was something she seemed to be able to answer easily and her smile lit up the place. "Yes, Christian. Very much so." She repeated his words back to him.

He knew what he was doing. He was manipulating the conversation, something his mother was much better at than he was, but he had to try. He veered back to his original question, thinking that if he knew, he could protect himself. But there was possibly no protection from Riley Zayat. Still, he asked, "Are you just out with me because you're attracted to me?"

She shook her head "no" and maybe the little extra time had been enough. "No Christian, I like you because you get me. I like that you're as smart as you are. You challenge me. So many men get intimidated, but not you, you let me be as smart or ignorant as I am and neither is bad. Some guys think I'm this little elementary school teacher and they treat me like I don't understand their big jobs. Then they see the text books on my shelf and freak out and run away. Maybe they realize too late how much of a nerd I am."

Christian laughed at her for that. "You're not too much of a nerd."

"See?" she pointed out. "That's exactly it. And yes, I'm attracted to you and I love that you're so honest. I always feel like what you say to me is real. I'm not always prepared for it, but I trust it. And that's a feeling that I haven't gotten from anyone else."

He was smiling, and thinking that was the best answer she could have given. But he wasn't finished, there was another thing he needed to know. "Can I ask you something else?"

The look on her face told him she heard the apprehension in his voice.

❧ 17 ❧

Riley nodded, not sure where this was going, but wanting to know next why *he* liked *her*—if they were asking deeper questions than they had been.

But what he said was, "There are a few things that I need to know aren't the reason."

Riley had no clue what was next, so she asked, "What are they?"

"My parents? My family name? Women have dated me in the past to try to get into the Mayfair family. I mean, if that's what you want, there are better routes..." He paused and thought, "My cousin Jackson needs a wife. Charlie's never home, so he'd make a great husband if you wanted the name."

He may or may not have been sarcastic, but Riley laughed anyway. Maybe it was partially relief that it wasn't anything she couldn't answer. She took another bite of her chicken and spanish rice. "I'm not from this town. I don't need to be a Mayfair. You can check that one off of your list."

He nodded. "Good. The other one I need to know is the money. I know my mother likes to tell everybody how much money I made and I've been dated for it in the past."

"Oh." Riley felt her mouth go round at the statement. It

made sense, and he wasn't wrong. One of the first things his mother had told her about him was how much money he had made. "Christian. It's not the money. I really don't care about the money. I have enough to pay my bills. I worked hard for it. And I like paying my own bills. There were times I wasn't sure I'd make that goal, and it feels good." She held her glass up, the second brand of cider sloshing a little as she gestured to the room. "I bought this place. No cosigner, all mine. I'm proud of that."

"I wasn't trying to insult you. I know that I'm smarter than the average person. I know that I make more money than the average person. I own a home that I paid cash for. I just don't want that to be a reason. I know a lot of women are looking to get married and have kids and have everything set up and... I just want you to be here for *me*." He took a breath and she could tell he was waiting on her response.

That was Christian: always raw, always real. Which might be what she liked about him best. "Christian, I didn't take it as an insult. And you're right, those things might be an obstacle." He hadn't said it in arrogance. He stated it as a fact, and she liked that. He didn't say he was rich—apparently, whatever his standards were, he wasn't there yet. But it was true, if Westerley was correct, that he had more money than the average guy in Breathless, then he might want to worry about it.

"Your mother does like to brag on you and it's sweet that she's so proud. But if I'm honest, when she told me how much money you made, I didn't really believe her."

"You thought my mother was lying?" he asked, almost incredulous.

"Never!" she replied, "but she was bragging on you. So I thought maybe she was exaggerating. Or maybe she'd heard one number somewhere, and maybe it was accurate at one point, but not anymore. I don't know, but I didn't put any stock in it."

He nodded at her. "That makes sense. My mother can exaggerate with the best of them."

Riley smiled. "I'll tell you what..." She grabbed a paper napkin that had come with the food and hopped up to get a pen.

Christian, for all his building a table at the last moment, actually had cloth napkins. She didn't. So she used the napkin with the restaurant logo embossed into the brown paper. Flipping it over, she wrote "Prenuptial Agreement" across the top.

I Riley Zayat, she filled in, *agree to split all holdings upon any divorce in the amounts that they were brought into the marriage. I further agree not to pursue alimony in any level and Child Support only as necessary.*

She turned the napkin around to face him. He'd been frowning as she wrote, but she asked, "What else does it need?"

"That's a prenuptial agreement, Riley." He was still frowning.

"I know." She smiled and shrugged as though it were no big deal. "And I know we're not there yet. But I wanted you to know that I'm not after your money. I just like you."

When he didn't have anything to add. She signed it boldly with a flourish.

"What's that?" he asked. "Your name's not Riley?"

"Oh no." She shook her head and handed the napkin over before going back to her dinner.

"I wondered. It sounded very American for someone with the last name Zayat."

"Nope. Not American. I am Raizel Shoshana. My mother wanted me to have an American sounding name, so she always called me Riley."

"It's beautiful. Is it Middle Eastern and Hebrew?"

She nodded as he picked up the napkin, held it up, and read it through once again. Then, right in front of her eyes, he shredded it.

"Hey!" she protested half-heartedly. "You just gave me a legal open door. I wrote you a prenup agreement so that you would know I'm not in it for the money."

He set the small pile of paper shreds beside him. "And now I know."

He looked her in the eyes again. It was one of the things she loved best about Christian.

Oh hell, she thought, she was in trouble here. Even just mentally, the words in her brain had changed from *like* to something more. In a bold attempt to cover up her realization and not blurt anything stupid about her feelings, she blurted something stupid on a different topic. "So, did you dye your hair?"

He rolled his eyes. "No, I told my sister I wouldn't dye it." He sighed. His hair was still the rich brown color from the week before. It didn't show any pool damage.

"Did you stop swimming?" Riley asked before she thought it all out. That wouldn't change his hair for a few months and she assumed he wouldn't have quit a sport or gym routine that he seemed to like.

Shaking his head, Christian made a face as though his hair was a distasteful topic. Riley found that just made her more interested. "It's some color-depositing conditioner. It's supposed to reverse all the damage the pool does. Technically, it's not dye. It's a loophole she roped me into."

She didn't want to laugh, but he was so uptight about it. "Well, it looks great. You get to keep your color and clearly, it's working."

His shoulders visibly untensed in front of her, even though he didn't say anything. For all his nonchalance, Christian just wanted to be accepted. Just like the rest of them. But he was some kind of smart Superman, stumbling around like a Clark Kent. Her heart tumbled a little further in her chest. She was a goner.

When dinner was over, she told him he couldn't drive yet. They'd split five ciders. It was over the course of several hours, but... it was a good excuse. They'd watched a tv show together. Or they'd started to. By the time Christian left, she'd had to button up her shirt and he'd had to put his back on.

Jesus, that swimmer-body was going to kill her. She was breathing heavy and could feel the bee-sting touch on her lips from their almost frantic, teenager-like make out session. The only reason they'd quit was because of some mumbling about "School tomorrow," and "I should probably go."

Riley was three seconds from just saying *yes*. She wanted this man. He made her feel alive and beautiful and smart and valued and... Jesus, she had to put her hand to her chest just to lock up the front door behind him. The feel of her fingers on the front of her blouse told her she'd buttoned it wrong. With a wry smile, she thanked whatever gods were watching that she wasn't going out in public.

Christian's shirt was a pullover, so if he stopped anywhere on the way home, at least he didn't have to worry. Unless he'd put it on inside out? Those soft, thermal tees had fast become her favorite thing to touch... until she'd touched bare skin tonight.

She headed through the unit, turning off lights and trying not to touch her lips or test if her cheeks were still overheated. But when she hit the bedroom, she pulled out the nightstand drawer and plucked out a condom.

Better check the expiration date. Then she smiled to see they weren't expired. She didn't think she had many more nights of shrugging this off because of timing or some sense of decorum. She was plummeting down the cliff side and there was nothing she could do about it.

❧ 18 ❧

Riley startled as Christian's phone rang Sunday morning.

He opened one sleepy green eye and looked at her as though this were somehow her fault. Riley still didn't have a voice, so she shook her head at him. As the phone rang again, he seemed to place it, rolled over and answered it with gravel in his voice.

She wondered if whoever was on the other end of the line—whoever might be calling on a Sunday morning—could hear that he wasn't at home. That he was in her bed. Naked.

Rolling over, Riley enjoyed all the little pulls and sore spots in her muscles. She felt almost as if she'd turned to liquid. He'd come over Friday night, this time later in the evening than usual.

She'd been growing desperate. Thanksgiving had screwed up the school schedule. He'd had family in town, his brother Charlie even came in from off the continent. Bailey Ann had talked about getting her father up and around for the holidays, though she was still struggling to get him to doctors and get the right diagnosis and even just to get him to take his damn medications.

Riley's own family had come to town, and they'd done up an *American Thanksgiving*, as her grandmother called it. They'd asked about men in her life, but she'd only said she was seeing someone. Saying the name "Christian Weaver" would have opened all kinds of conversations that would have overshadowed whether the turkey should be baked or fried. Plain ham or brown sugar brine? Did Grandma's traditional latkes count as the potatoes at American Thanksgiving? Riley wasn't ready to share it yet, and she'd held on for the whirlwind of vacation time and family all at once.

She'd not gotten to see Christian but once, and only for a coffee. Then this week, as school had started in again, his brother had lingered. Charlie's mere presence demanded Christian's time. She couldn't begrudge him a brother he rarely saw anymore, but she was dying over here. "Christian, come out with me tonight!"

"I have to work," he'd protested when she asked him to go out for dinner and a movie with her as they cleaned up after the last class of the week.

She hadn't played fair. She'd worn a wrap dress and, while he shelved the last of the projects, she'd climbed up on the edge of her desk and sat there waiting for him. "You don't have to work." She'd used her coyest voice.

"I have to work," he'd protested again, but this time he'd looked up, and she moved her knees just a little and she'd watched as his breath hitched.

It was so wrong. She was at her office, which was an elementary school, for God's sakes, but this man did things to her.

"Come here." She'd crooked a finger at him and smiled when he narrowed his eyes but came closer. Riley had reached up around his neck and pulled him down for a kiss. Wrapping her legs around him, she kept him trapped. There was a disciplinary hearing in her future if anyone looked in the door right then, but no one ever did. So she kissed him with tongue.

It backfired on her, hard, when she felt his thumb creeping up the inside of her thigh. Slow circles driving her mad and making her foolishly believe that she could probably get away with getting laid right here on her desk.

They'd both jolted upright and jumped apart.

Yeah, she thought, reaching up to check her hair, *we don't look guilty at all*. But she wasn't going to last much longer, or she really would wind up throwing him down on her desk and getting herself fired from her dream job. "When can you come over tonight?"

Did he catch what she was really asking?

He pulled out his phone as he turned away, almost as though he couldn't quite look at her and get anything done. "I'll get you at seven thirty." He held up the screen and told her he'd take her to the movie he was pointing to.

Riley agreed. So maybe he hadn't caught her hint. Hmmm.

When the movie was over, and he'd deposited her on her doorstep, she grabbed the front of his shirt and tugged him inside with her.

"Oh, thank God. I thought you were going to send me home," he'd whispered the words between biting kisses and tugs at her clothing.

"I thought you'd misunderstood my invitation," she'd almost growled back.

He shook his head. "You said you wanted to go see that movie. You said you wanted to see it while it's still in the theaters and it's almost gone."

She pulled her head back a little and looked him in the eyes.

"Did you like it?" he asked, but he was killing her.

"Yes." It wasn't about the movie. It was that he'd *remembered*. She was in a load of trouble, but right then, Riley grabbed him and pulled him into the living room. The rest passed in a blur of popped buttons, peeled shirts, and wild touches.

She hadn't been sure she wasn't going to have to say, "I want to have sex with you!" but there she was, splayed across his lap, facing away from him. His mouth was on her neck as her head lolled to the side to give him access to more skin. Her shirt hung open and his was gone. One of his large hands cupped her breast and made her gasp needy little noises.

He'd whispered, "You're beautiful" as he touched her, and the words had run through her like a freight train. She'd dated players and never quite trusted them. Christian meant every word, she had no doubt. Whether she was empirically beautiful or not, *he believed it.*

As she'd sucked in a breath at his words, he'd popped the snap on her jeans and reached in. His fingers found her wet, then writhing as he touched her. He'd driven her crazy, whispering in her ear, "Come for me."

He had no idea how he was killing her. How he was tying her to him. How hard and fast she was falling.

"I like watching you." The whispered words in her ear were coming from so far away, she was so close.

Riley barely managed to open her eyes and see what he meant. The TV was off, the dark panel acting as a pale mirror. Her mouth fell open and she saw herself as he did, a goddess across his lap, legs wide, breasts falling out of her shirt and into his hand, moving to the rhythm he stroked.

Her voice had crescendoed as she shattered in his arms. She saw him in the reflection, watching her, eyes dark with his own need. When she could move again, when he'd turned her around and kissed her sweetly, softly, she'd said, "Oh no. This is not over."

Christian Weaver had given her a wicked grin she didn't even know he possessed.

Though she was boneless, he was not, and she found herself being tossed onto her bed before she could have moved herself. If coming apart in his arms hadn't overwhelmed her, making love to him did.

He didn't get up and leave after. He'd simply whispered, "Tell me I get to stay."

Riley had curled into him and held on. That had been late Friday night. Since then, she'd gotten out of the bed to eat, shower, and christen some of her furniture. She had no idea how she was going to get to class tomorrow. How she would talk to anyone without thinking of Christian Weaver's tongue on her—

"Let me ask."

His hand at her shoulder brought her back to reality. The look on his face told her that this call was not about anything sexy. Sighing, she raised her eyebrows at him, words failing.

"Sunday dinner? With my family?"

She blinked. "Tonight?" She pointed downward as though the bed itself were Sunday.

But he nodded at her and mouthed the word "Please."

Riley had been two heartbeats away from refusing. Surely there was a good excuse she could come up with. It hit her then: Christian had never made an excuse to her. If he didn't want to do something—like spend his time in a noisy restaurant—he said so. He didn't lie or offer fake reasons to get out of things. She owed him no less than the same.

"If you want me there." She whispered it back, hoping that whomever was on the phone didn't hear.

He nodded at her as he spoke into the phone. "We'll both be there. Five. Yes." He hung up the phone and said, "If I can handle Sunday dinner with my family, you can, too."

She'd only nodded and tried to calculate how many hours they had before she had to get out of this bed.

"We have to make deviled eggs. I always bring deviled eggs."

"Okay, what do I need to bring?"

"Yourself. I know you already know most of them, but I want them to meet my girlfriend."

Oh shit. How could she say no to that? "Then I guess we have deviled eggs to make," she said out loud, but inside she was wondering how to hold her heart together if he ever left her.

✤ 19 ✤

Your belt must go the same direction as the button placket on your pants.

CHRISTIAN FOUGHT TO KEEP THE FLUTTERING DOWN IN HIS chest.

Sunday dinner sometimes made him nervous. Sometimes it was good, easy, simple, and he knew what he was getting. But not tonight.

He didn't know if his mother had thought this through, or just invited Riley on a whim. Maybe she'd heard that he was sleeping with his new girlfriend and, thus, it was serious enough to meet the family. Christian did not doubt the possibility of his mother having those kinds of powers.

But he worried, would only his own immediate family be there? That would mean his mom and dad, his sister, himself and Riley. Charlie was off the continent again, so that helped limit numbers. It also helped limit the possibility that his little brother would charm the pants off his girlfriend.

Not that Charlie would do any such thing on purpose. He

couldn't help it. Looks and personality-wise, Christian and Charlie could not have been more different. And, though he hated to admit it, Christian was glad his brother wouldn't be there.

If his mother hadn't planned this out thoroughly, this could potentially be one of the big family dinners. Christian had been too flustered to ask. But it would mean his cousin Jax and his two small daughters, and Bailey Ann would be there with her dad—his Uncle Con. Also Uncle Dex and Aunt GiGi. He loved them all, but it was more than Christian was willing to deal with the first time he brought Riley. *He should have asked.*

Riley exhibited no qualms about meeting the family, nor about meeting them this early, nor even about the fact that he had qualms. In fact, she'd just reached up and pulled a bottle of wine from her cupboard to bring along. She smiled at him and waved the bottle in front of him. "I don't think I can buy a bottle on Sunday. But I have this and it should do."

"I told you, you don't need to bring anything."

"Look," she told him. "This is the *South* and your cousin seems to think that I'm an actual Southern Belle. I'm not going to ruin that perception. I would never show up empty handed! Also, I'd love to grab some flowers this afternoon."

She'd grinned up at him as though he might have told her "no." So he nodded at her, feeling the frown form between his eyebrows. It was something else to stop for, something else to do when he was already a little anxious, but they were up and dressed and he'd calculated out plenty of time.

He'd messed up his whole plan. He hadn't intended to spend the entire weekend in bed with Riley. He thought he'd go grocery shopping Saturday, make his deviled eggs Sunday morning and be way ahead of time and ready to walk in his parents' door at five p.m. *by himself.*

This was a bit of a wrench in the system, but he hoped it was actually a good wrench. As much as he was anxious about all the ways things could go wrong, there were far more ways for them to go right. He was excited and hopeful that having Riley there was a good thing.

Taking the girlfriend or boyfriend to Sunday dinner was a Mayfair rite of passage. He'd watched all his cousins go through it, some of them more than once, but this was the first time he'd brought anyone home.

"Do you want me to drop you back home?" he asked her after he had tried to figure out if they were low on anything they needed. "Or do you want to come with me and we'll make the deviled eggs together?"

Riley had looked around her living area and up to the ceiling as though she could see into her bedroom above their heads. "I can come with you. It's probably easier to go straight over. Right?"

He'd nodded at the practicality, but he still wasn't quite ready to relax about it. At the store, they'd grabbed fresh eggs and he'd bought her favorite ice cream for his own freezer. She'd raised one eyebrow at him, but didn't protest.

Just before they hit the checkout line, she straightened up suddenly. "Wait!" Heading to the floral section, she picked a large bouquet, a glass vase and a roll of ribbon.

"Don't you think that's overkill?"

"Nope. I don't think so," she replied as simply as she could.

Suddenly, he wondered if she was thinking along the same lines he was. Was it possible that Riley was trying to make a good impression because she wanted to come back? Did she see this as an ongoing thing?

His heart thumped at the idea, but he didn't ask. He stayed quiet the whole drive home.

In his galley style kitchen, they worked back to back. He'd thought it would be too small for two people, but they maneuvered easily in tune with each other.

"Scissors?" she asked.

"Drawer. There." He pointed

He put the eggs in the pot and set the timer.

"Where do I put these?" She trimmed the stems from the flowers and held the leftover pieces out in her hand.

"Compost." He pointed again. He was trying to shake the jitters he was feeling, but he couldn't quite quell them. "I put the list of things that can go in on the lid."

Riley stood and read it for a moment. She'd been here before, so she knew about the compost pile, but they hadn't worked in his kitchen.

At least that was working well, he thought. Aside from a few questions, they moved like they knew what they were doing. But then she opened drawers, closing them and going to the next one, obviously looking for something.

"What's your organization system?" she finally asked.

He pointed to each drawer in turn. "Slicing, scooping, table service." It wasn't the usual way people did it, he knew. But he thought it made perfect sense and it grouped them in the right amounts. All his drawers closed without catching and weren't the odd jumble his mother and sister seemed to prefer.

Riley didn't ask again. He figured it was a testament to a solid organization. Their easy harmony continued without them talking until she held up the vase complete with artfully arranged flowers, flower food in the water, and the big ribbon tied around it in a professional looking bow. It was a talent he hadn't known she had.

"My mother will love it," he said even as his thoughts tumbled. He'd just been thinking how well he understood this woman, how well they'd functioned together. But a bouquet of flowers was catching him off guard. What else didn't he know about her?

And how much did he need to know?

"Good!" Her declaration and smile showed she was oblivious to his churning thoughts.

Was that okay? Did she need to know when he was upset? She picked up on it a lot, but this afternoon she'd not seemed to notice at all. Were they not as much in sync as he'd thought? Or did it not matter as much as he'd thought?

Once he got the eggs in an ice bath, he set the timer and begged Riley to make love to him. He needed it. Needed to connect and make sure they were still the unit he'd thought. But his mouth only said, "One more time. Come on."

Her mouth replied with a smile and, "You're an animal." But her arms wrapped around his neck and she pushed up on her toes so she could press her mouth to his and her body down the length of him.

The tension drained out of him. How long would it be that he would need her like this? Need this reassurance that they were solid? But again, those scary thoughts didn't come out in his words.

"I don't know when I'll see you again," he murmured against her mouth, apparently surprising her. "I've got meetings all week. I'm handing in the upgrade to the app and I'll have to clean up anything they need."

"Are the meetings online?"

He nodded. "But I don't know quite when yet. I'll be on call."

"Then we'll work around it." She pressed her lips to his, sinking into the kiss.

His heart settled in his chest then. It was always surprising to him when he didn't realize just how uptight he'd gotten waiting for an answer, but then Riley would say something, and everything would loosen. Christian relaxed into her hold and tugged her down the hallway to his room this time.

An hour later, the egg timer woke him up. He popped out of bed feeling much better, pulled on his jeans, and headed downstairs.

"I didn't know you own jeans." Riley commented, apparently watching his ass as he went,

"These are soft," he hollered back as he heard her laughing behind him and went to get the eggs.

In a moment she joined him. Everything was perfect, dinner

didn't matter, because however it turned out, Riley was with him. Then, she looked over his shoulder as he stirred the egg yolks.

"There's no pickle relish here." She was looking at his lineup of ingredients on the counter.

Christian stopped stirring. "Pickle relish is an abomination."

She stared for a moment. "I'm not sure if you're serious."

For a moment, he thought about it. "I kind of am. No pickle relish in the deviled eggs."

"But there's at least pickle relish in your house?"

"No, there's no pickle relish in my house. It's an abomination."

Riley stared back at him. "Deviled eggs *without* pickle relish are an abomination."

❧ 2 0 ❧

C hristian sat at his spot around the big table but hung back from the conversation.

Luckily, it was only his immediate family at dinner. However, Riley was fresh meat and his mother and sister—and even his father—were peppering her with questions. Christian was apparently not needed in this conversation.

"Where did you grow up?" Carlisle asked with an almost-convincingly casual air as she buttered a roll. At least she didn't ask, "Who are your people?"

Riley smiled, complimented the green beans and told them about Northern California.

"Why did you go into teaching?" his father asked. Christian wondered if his mother had fed the old man that question. She couldn't pull it off after having volunteered in Riley's room for several years.

Her answer was relatively rote until Carlisle pushed.

"Wait, so they aren't done testing once they get into the gifted program? Isn't it enough to be gifted?"

Riley shook her head, seemingly unfazed by the questions, or the follow-ups, or even the follow-ups to the follow-ups.

"I know a lot of people are against all the standardized testing." She gestured with a spoon, seeming perfectly comfortable in her spot at another family's table. "And there's definitely too much, so I try to keep it to a minimum. But I'm constantly going over their scores and I have to call the parents and have conferences—"

Carlisle tipped her head. "The scores are too high?"

Riley laughed at her. "You might think so, given the way your brother probably tests. But, no. One of my big jobs is to help boost the children in their weak areas."

At last Christian joined the conversation, confused. He'd been in her classroom a good number of times now, but... "I thought your job was to nurture whatever they were gifted in. You're helping Jacob sew and design an entire costume series. Lisa Lynn is programming a game for everyone to play. Those are the areas where they have superior talent."

"Right," Riley answered looking up at him.

She had three deviled eggs sitting on the side of her plate, nestled against rice and peas. As he watched, Carlisle glanced at the eggs and then turned to look at Christian, her eyebrows raised as though to ask, "How did that happen?"

He knew she'd spotted the small green flecks in the centers of Riley's eggs. But he didn't answer her unspoken question; he was still waiting for Riley.

"The problem with most gifted kids—even if they get into a gifted program—" she explained to the table at large, "—is that we tend to teach to the idea that, when they're gifted, everything else is okay. But it's often not. Most gifted kids have weak areas just like everyone else. But, because they're gifted, those weak areas often don't even get addressed the way they would in a regular classroom."

It hit Christian then, her idea barreling through his head and changing the way he would look at everything else in his life. He'd not been prepared for an epiphany at Sunday dinner. He could feel his breathing change with the sudden understanding that Riley could have been talking about him. His eyes flicked up and caught his mother glancing over with a frown on her face.

This was exactly what they had missed with him.

He was gifted and they'd nurtured those gifts. His parents bought him the best computers, got him tutoring, advanced him grade levels past his peers, and completely ignored that he didn't interact well with others. He'd had weak areas as a kid and here he was in his thirties and they'd never been addressed.

Riley kept smiling and talking. "It's my job to help fill in the gap so they can live their best life, get their best jobs, and make the best use of their gifts. For example, if Jacob can sew like the devil, but he can't work with numbers, then he can't give an esti-mate for costume design and get a job with a Hollywood studio running the costuming department. If Lisa Lynn can program an award-winning game, but she can't keep her temper together for long enough to have a solid conversation or correct what her employer needs, she can't hold a job. Interestingly enough, the gifted pieces will often take care of themselves if given room to grow." She looked around the table, and Christian saw she had a rapt audience. "I think the bulk of my work is filling in the weak spaces."

The way his mother was looking at him, Christian knew she was thinking the same things he was. He wanted to tell her that it was okay and that she'd done her best. Clearly, none of them had known when he was small that he needed a teacher like Riley to help backfill the missing pieces.

The whole table had a pause for a moment, almost as if noticing as a group that they had stepped in something. It was Carlisle who jumped in to fill the gap. "Christian. What do you want for your birthday?"

That sparked Riley. "Is your birthday coming up?"

Damn Carlisle, he thought. He didn't like talking about his birthday. He wasn't a big fan of his birthday and his whole family knew it. He also didn't like the sudden realization—just when he'd been thinking that weekend how perfect he and Riley were together—that they didn't even know each other's birthdays.

"He was born on Christmas." His mother piped up, and Christian almost groaned. Not this again. *Yes, this again.*

"Best Christmas present ever!" his father added.

"It's why we named him Christian." Westerley talked over her husband.

Once again, Christian wasn't even needed in this conversation.

"I have an idea what to get for you," Carlisle at least addressed him. "But if there's something you really want. Let me know. It may override my plans."

Christian wasn't quite sure how to take that. Usually Carlisle wound up getting him whatever it was he said he wanted. Even though she always said she "had plans" he'd never seen them. Usually, his recommendations were some item that he just remembered he needed so that she would have a thing to get him. Otherwise he often wound up with a gift card to the nearest computer store.

"My blender broke," he blurted out. Well, now he was going to have to wait several weeks to see if Carlisle got him a blender. It was easier just to buy the model he wanted himself. He didn't know why he hadn't done it yet, but he was stuck now.

The dinner conversation shifted once more, swirling around Riley and her past and her parents.

Christian had piped up once to volunteer her full name, which he'd only recently learned. "It's a beautiful name." He told his family, wondering if it was obvious how much he thought the name suited its bearer.

Eventually, things wound down and plates were carried to the sink and he'd left to check his old desk and see if he could find the disks he'd left. He'd told the kids about five-and-a-half-inch-floppies but they had no frame of reference. He wanted to show them several old disks and he thought he still had some here. As he came back down the stairs, he heard voices and stopped.

"What was that you were carrying on the way in?" Carlisle was asking Riley.

"Deviled eggs." Riley answered as though it was obvious. She'd had a glass container with her four abominable eggs separate from the others. She'd called him an egg racist. He'd agreed.

Now he could almost hear Carlisle's face scrunching into that thinking position.

She was calculating that he'd clearly bought pickle relish for the eggs. And she was right. He'd walked down to the corner store and paid too much for too little of a condiment he'd never eat. He'd set aside four eggs and—after he filled all the others with the good stuff—he'd mixed in pickle relish and set the other four aside for Riley.

Carlisle now told his new girlfriend, "He's in love with you."

Christian had stopped dead on the staircase, almost plastering himself to the wall, wondering if he could hide there forever.

Why was Carlisle saying that? And why wasn't Riley answering?

It took a moment, but he heard Riley's voice defending him. "It was just deviled eggs."

Christian crossed his fingers, but apparently not quickly enough.

"Deviled eggs are his specialty," Carlisle told his girlfriend. "And he hates pickle relish to the point of a passion."

Shut up, Carlisle! He wished hard, but it didn't work. He had no such mental powers. Desperately wanting to end the conversation, he trumped down the remaining steps, letting them know he was coming.

Luckily, that brought Carlisle's little oil spill of secrets to a halt. He held up the disks he'd found. "I think I'm ready to go."

Riley had looked at him a little oddly as they gathered their things and headed out the door. They managed to not speak almost the entire way back to her house where he dropped her off without going inside.

"I need to sleep alone tonight. You know I didn't sleep much this weekend. You should go back to your place."

He felt his heart clench as he nodded and kissed her goodbye on her front step. Turning away, he climbed back into his car, his thoughts more of a jumble than they'd been before they left for dinner.

Was it because of what Carlisle had said? Or was it simply because—as Riley protested—she needed to be up and ready for Monday mornings class?

He didn't know.

And he didn't know how to find out.

❧ 21 ❧

"That was excellent, Molly!" Riley told the third grader. Honestly, Christian had probably done half the original programming and he'd stepped in several times during the presentation to make the little robot dog go the correct way more than once. Riley wanted to say, "That was excellent, Christian!" but it was Molly's project and Christian was *merely* her assistant.

It was Wednesday afternoon and the children were about to head back to their classrooms. Riley could feel every minute of this week in her bones. The projects finally finishing up between this week and the next.

Several students—like Seven—had completed theirs weeks earlier and then helped other students. But next week was the last week they could present—which meant next week was the last week Christian would be in her classroom.

Not wanting to get overwhelmed, Riley had tried to space the projects out, so there would only be a few remaining. It was a relief to see all the work come to a satisfying end. It was also a relief to have her room clear out.

She waved goodbye as the kids headed back to their homerooms. Her mind turned to wondering what she would do when

Christian was no longer a part of her class. She'd grown far too used to having him here.

He'd still be part of her life, she thought. But even that wasn't quite as settled as she'd like. This week had just felt a little odd. While everything had been wonderful, she had a small worry nagging just under her breastbone.

Riley turned to him now as he put the toys away, comfortable in the room and not needing her instruction much anymore. "Hey," she called to him softly, and watched as he turned and looked at her.

He'd had a dose of apprehension coloring his eyes this whole week, and she'd wondered what it was about. He hadn't volunteered anything, but they really hadn't had time. They hadn't even managed their usual coffee shop outing.

He'd been on deadline and generally not available. Now, she walked up to him and grabbed the front of his shirt, stood up on her tiptoes and pressed her lips to his. "Come over tonight... Stay with me."

He was shaking his head no. As always, his expression gave nothing away. Though Riley hadn't learned how to read him better, she had learned to not be nervous until he said his peace. "My meeting will run late. It's with people on the Pacific coast. So the time zones are off and I don't know when it will end."

"Then come over when it ends." She tried to latch onto something more concrete.

"Why don't you come to me?"

She nodded yes, and for the first time, hope flared in the center of her chest. He wasn't just putting her off. He'd simply been busy. She had been a little crazy thinking about what his sister said. It had been several days and Riley had all but discounted it. He wasn't in love with her. They were too new. But as she watched he pulled the key off his chain and tucked it into her palm.

"Let yourself in when you get there. Come by eight? I'll still be in a meeting, but you can make yourself at home, and as soon as I'm done, I'll come find you."

Frowning down at her palm, Riley wondered, *Had he just given her his key?*

But she had more pressing concerns. "Do I stay over?"

"Please," he whispered against her lips as he kissed her again.

"Should I bring an overnight bag or go home in the morning?" The logistics of the back and forth was a pain in the ass, but it was better to know than to wake up late and not be ready for work on time.

"Do whatever is more comfortable for you, but stay over with me."

It was hard to argue with that, she thought and curled the key tighter in her hand. One last time she gave him a sweet peck on the mouth before he left again.

Sighing into the empty room, Riley wished it was different, but it was hard to complain. She was on a nine to five schedule; he wasn't. Yet he'd managed to carve out time for her classroom for the past several months.

Only after he was gone, did she look down at her hand and think again that he'd just given her his house key. Surely, he had a backup somewhere. Christian wasn't the kind of man to make that mistake. So she put it into her wallet and told herself she'd wait until she got home to call.

She barely made it into the car before she dialed the phone. Angelia was who she would normally have turned to, but Bailey Ann was the better bet in this instance. At least she was until she answered the phone, and Riley realized her mistake.

She just called her boyfriend's *cousin* to ask about sleeping over with him. Well, too late now, she thought as Bailey Ann's voice filled the air. "Hi, Riley. What's up?"

"Well, I was calling you for good Southern girl advice and then I realized I was being a bad Belle."

Bailey Ann replied, "I'm not sure how you do that. But tell me."

"I'm asking for advice about sleeping over at a man's house and that man happens to be—"

"Oh, my *cousin*," she replied. Riley could hear the grin in her friend's voice even through the phone line.

"Yes ma'am."

"Well, you should do it. I'd love to have the opportunity to sleep over anywhere and I know for a fact Christian's wild about you."

The melancholy behind the words gave Riley pause. For all her appearance of being together, maybe Bailey Ann was lonely in the big house with the grumpy father who seemed determined to follow his wife to the afterlife. It was one of those things Riley thought everyone saw, but no one mentioned. Bailey Ann was stuck being the good daughter.

"That's actually not my question," Riley turned her thoughts back.

"Oh, so this is not a *will you or won't you.*"

"No, we've already proven that I will."

At least that made her friend laugh. Bailey Ann could use more of that. "Well, damn girl. Tell me the question."

"It's a weeknight and I'm heading over to his place. Late. If I pack a bag and then leave from his house in the morning is everyone going to know? And if they do, is that any worse than leaving from his house to come back to my house to get ready?" Riley did not want to start rumors in a small town where she was an elementary teacher. But she was going to stay over.

There was silence from the other end of the line, and she felt her nerves kick up.

"Oh God, is it that bad? Like I can't even stay over? Because I already did, and if that's the case then the whole town already thinks I'm a slut! But I'm *not*. Because I'm just—"

"Hush," Bailey Ann interrupted. "It's not that. I was just trying to think it through. I actually don't believe there's any real difference. What happens probably depends on how nosy his neighbors are. If you've already been over there, then whatever gossip is going to get spread about tomorrow has probably already been spread. Has he been at your place, too?"

"That would be an affirmative," Riley replied.

"Then you do what you want." Bailey Ann told her. "Nobody has any right to say otherwise."

Riley took a deep breath and let out some of her anxiety. Her feelings for Christian sometimes crowded out everything else. "Thank you. I just needed a sounding board."

"Glad to be of service, uh—"

It sounded as though she was going to add something else to the end of that. But Riley was guessing anything that Bailey Ann might have said would probably sound bad given that the man in question was her cousin. A good *don't do anything I wouldn't do* didn't have the same meaning. Bailey Ann never finished her cut off thought, and Riley thanked her and let her go.

Her breathing was much easier now than it had been when she'd left the school. After eating dinner, she headed over to Christian's. The front door was locked, and it was exciting—even though it shouldn't be—to let herself into his house with a key she already had.

Setting her bag inside the front door, she locked it and heard his voice coming from the office. He was clearly still in the middle of his meeting. She didn't want to stick her head in the door because his desk was up against the wall and the camera might reveal her in the background. But she was not above standing in the hallway and listening in.

"No, you can't do that." Christian's voice rang through the walls. It was just like him, not softening the blow, only giving pure honesty. No was no from him. Yes was yes.

"Then we'll write the extra code ourselves," the voice replied and Riley only wondered for a moment what they were discussing.

"I won't create an app that allows for that kind of online abuse. It's already a feature to not accept cryptocurrency."

"Why not? It's valid currency, and we want an app that's usable in a variety of situations."

"No, you don't. You don't want to sell a matching app into the dark web for human trafficking." Christian protested and Riley almost gasped. Of course, he was already aware that his work could be used for illicit purposes and he was fighting against it. It was only news to her.

"Many legitimate transactions involve cryptocurrency. We need to support it."

Christian countered again, swiftly, making her heart squeeze with his conviction. "Legitimate transactions accept almost every other form of currency. There's no reason to honor cryptocurrency. While blockchain technology remains the currency of the dark web, I won't support it with my app."

"Then we'll alter it."

"No, it's registered. And I built in traps if you try. You're more than welcome to refuse payment and break the contract. We'll simply take my app out of the equation and you can build your own." There was something in the way he said it that let everyone know he was more than willing to take his toys and go home if this company wasn't willing to play in an ethical manner.

Truly, it didn't sound like the company *wanted* to be unethical, just that they were wanting to offer up the option and they didn't really care it might be misused.

Christian disagreed.

Lord, that was a turn on.

Riley also gathered from the conversation that his threat to take his toys home was bigger than it sounded. Chances were no one else would be able to get them the kind of platform that he could. That was disturbingly hot. Riley was fanning herself and smiling as she headed down the hall.

Opening his fridge, she looked for a drink. One of the beers called to her, and she decided to go ahead and drink it since, clearly, he wasn't going to. She was sitting on the couch watching

TV when he finally came out and kissed her hello before sitting beside her. But she didn't wait more than just a moment.

She wanted to jump him, but she had to ask her question. Reaching into her pocket, she pulled out his house key. "Do you want this back?"

❧ 22 ❧

"*I'm not in charge here,*" *is Belle code for* "*they're doing it wrong.*"

LATER THAT NIGHT, SATED AND HAPPY THAT SHE WAS expected to keep his key, Riley curled into Christian. The feel of him, the warmth of a man in bed with her, the soft rustle as he moved beside her were all things she'd quickly become accustomed to. It was now the nights they weren't together that felt off. Since it was a Thursday, she was glad he was at her place. That way she could get up early, get ready, and head out to school without too much trouble. He could sleep in and meet her at Brighton in the afternoon.

His arm tightened around her and she realized he'd not yet fallen asleep.

She spoke into the dark space around her. "It sounded like that talk about your app broke down."

He nodded. She didn't see it, but she felt the movement. "Once I made it clear I wouldn't use any blockchain technology, they decided to 'step away' and 'have a discussion.'"

She could hear the air quotes in his voice. "Does it bother

you? That they might decide not to use it after you've done all this work?"

This time, she felt him shake his head. "It's a good app. It's a base platform that now does even more than it used to. They commissioned the additions, so they have first rights to it, but if they refuse it then it all reverts back to me and I can sell it somewhere else. So I'm not that concerned."

Riley hesitated to ask, but she wanted to know. "How much money would you make when you sell it?" Then she'd almost choked when he gave her the answer.

If he picked up on her reaction, he didn't show it, and a few minutes later he was asleep. It took her a while longer to get her mind to let go of the fact that he was living on a different plane than she was—in many different ways. Their work was so different just in what it was and how it was delivered. He was exhausted from staying up late to meet deadlines. His eyes blurry from checking code and adding features the company was coming up with at the last minute. She was on a regular nine-to-five—almost—with children. Her salary was a fraction of his. Their lives were so different. But here he was, in bed with her, and it felt *right*.

Despite sleeping through her leaving in the morning almost without even twitching, Christian showed up on time to her classroom. He was awake and smiling and despite all his other work, he was invested in the kids. With a smile that said he wanted to greet her in a way that wasn't appropriate in the class-room, he dove in. The whole class was helping to get the last several projects done the following week.

On Friday night he surprised her with concert tickets.

"Oh my god, Christian, these are so expensive." The seats were down on the floor. Not far back from the stage, the kind of ticket she'd never buy herself.

"They weren't that bad," he offered, but she was looking at the ticket and it had the price stamped on it. She could see exactly how much they'd cost.

She raised an eyebrow at him.

He shrugged at her, but when she continued to stare at him, he said, "Fine. So they cost more than you can afford."

"They don't cost more than I can afford." She could have bought them, but it would have strained her budget. Hard. Hmmmm. Maybe they really did cost more than she could afford.

"So I bought them and I would like you to go with me." He was still looking at her as though she should just say "thank you." And she should.

Though she nodded, Riley found herself in a moral dilemma. He'd bought dinner more often than she had. He drove more often than she had, therefore buying more of the gas. She brought some of that up. "I can't have you paying for everything."

"I get that." He shook his head again, as though to say that he did get it, but it wasn't really going to change anything. "Look, if we each put in a corresponding percentage of our earnings that seems fair to me."

"It does seem fair," Riley conceded, "and I think it would be fair if we were anywhere near the same stratosphere in our earnings. But the problem is your ten percent and my ten percent are so far off. You'd still wind up paying for almost everything."

"Yes."

She almost sighed. That was Christian: Her math was correct, so what was the problem?

But he had a few other points. "And while you're making house payments, I'm not. All I'm doing is paying bills: Heating, Air Conditioning, that kind of thing. I barely even have credit cards to cover and I pay them off at the end of each month."

Must be nice, but she didn't say it out loud. As he spoke, a little knot of jealousy formed at the base of her throat. It took a moment to remind herself that she was fine and she knew it. Exactly as she'd told him before, she had signed for her home on her own. She could cover her bills. She was putting money into retirement savings and doing well. But not if she was buying concert tickets like this or paying off her credit cards at the end of each month.

"I don't know what to do with this." She held the tickets up.

"Well," he said, "you give them to the person at the arena entrance and then they run their little clicker and it makes a beep and you get into the concert."

"Don't be sarcastic."

With a sigh, Christian turned and looked at her. "What do you want me to say? Do you want to just not go, and I'll scalp my tickets at the last minute? Do you want me to go by myself?"

She shook her head. "I really like this band. And I *really* want to go! There are just no good answers here."

Now he was getting irritated at her. "There are plenty of good answers! The good answers are: let me buy the concert tickets. It's not a budget problem for me and you get to see a great concert. Maybe you want to buy the concessions or dinner beforehand?"

She thought about it for a moment. "I can and I don't mind doing it. But even that is going to limit how much I can participate. I do fine, but I'm living on a teacher's salary."

This time his head tilted, and something softened in his eyes. "I understand. You can live fine on that. I know you're saving and that's really important—so don't mess with that. You shouldn't be penalized because you picked a more noble profession than I did."

A snort almost came out of her nose at that one. "I'm not sure either of us *picked* these professions. It's just what we're good at. Where we fit."

"Exactly." He looked at her as though he'd just caught her in a trap. "You didn't pick what you're good at. Neither did I. It's just a random roll of the dice and you shouldn't be penalized for it. Let me provide some entertainment."

In the end, he won because the fact was he wasn't taking her out to fancy dinners every night. They ate tacos or cooked at home as much as anything. And he wasn't buying her expensive concert tickets all the time. In fact, she hadn't balked at all at the band several weeks before, because they'd been playing a hole-in-the-wall bar and the relatively unknown band had cost five dollars a ticket. So it wasn't as if he was trying to impress her with his money. He must have simply wanted to see this band badly enough to drive into Atlanta on a Friday night.

Before the concert, when the check came, he softly laid his hand over the ticket. At least the waiter had graciously set it on the table between them instead of just assuming the man had all the money—even if that would be correct in this situation.

Christian looked up at her. "This is yours if you want it. But I'd love if you let me pay for it, and you put this into your retirement savings."

That was exactly where it would have come from. Had he calculated it out? Figured out what her paycheck and her home were worth? She didn't doubt that he could. Though for Christian it wouldn't have been anything he researched, just something obvious that his amazing brain put together.

As wonderful as it was, it concerned her. It wasn't Christian's fault that he dramatically outearned her. And it wasn't his fault either that her mother seemed to think Riley should marry for stability. That a rich husband was a good husband. Riley had spent most of her life preparing to buck her mother's old-school ideas. She never wanted to be a dependent wife. It would kill her.

Christian was asking no such thing of her, but her own deeply embedded feelings were balking at the idea.

If that was the only thing, she told herself she might have been able to let it go. But it wasn't. The man volunteered in her classroom. What did she give back to him? How did she improve his life? She didn't buy him things. She didn't help with his work —she *couldn't*. She didn't even cook most of the time.

How long could she stay in a relationship so lopsided?

23

Christian turned the omelet with a precision he was proud of. It was a new skill acquired after moving to Breathless. He'd gotten a quick lesson from his mother without having to explain that he was trying to impress a woman... with breakfast.

The omelets were an attempt to help smooth over what must have been a snafu last night. He didn't think so, but there was a change in Riley's reaction when he'd told her he loved her.

It wasn't clear if the fact that he'd said it while he was inside her was a problem. Now, he tilted the pan and watched as the eggs ran. Riley would like mushrooms, but he wasn't about to make them for her. He didn't know how. But he'd also forgone the green peppers out of solidarity.

Sniffing at the air, he tested the bottom of the omelet and pulled it from the heat. Turning the pan, he slid the eggs out and neatly folded them onto the plate. He was pouring in the scrambled egg mix for the second omelet as Riley came out of the bedroom.

He almost missed adding the ham and cheese to the mix because he was looking at her. She'd thrown on one of his t-shirts and it was hitting just low enough to make him want to find out if she'd put on underwear or if all she had on in addition to his shirt were the slouchy socks.

When she raised her hand to run her fingers through her hair, he watched as the hem pulled up enough to reveal—oh, sweet Jesus, nope.

"Hey." He worked to drag his brain out of the gutter, but the gutter seemed to be easy access these days. "That omelet's for you."

She padded over to him, leaned up and kissed him on the cheek before grabbing her plate from the counter. Riley still hadn't said anything, but she grabbed silverware from his drawer and he noticed she pulled an extra set for him.

By the time he made it to the table she'd eaten almost a third of her omelet, but still hadn't said anything. If it were him, he wouldn't have thought anything, but this was Riley. So he waited.

A few moments later, she took what turned out to be her last bite and stood up. "That was really good."

Unable to untangle the expression on her face, Christian grew more worried by the moment. With a far too fast swallow, he opened his mouth to ask, but Riley was already at the counter, her plate with the remains of her breakfast now resting by the sink. "I need to get dressed and head home."

Again, there was no tone in her voice. But was it because it wasn't there? Or because it was, but he just wasn't capable of distinguishing what it meant?

She was heading down the hall before he could ask.

Still confused, Christian took one more bite before he decided that he couldn't afford to wait. Setting his fork on the counter, he pushed back his seat and turned. There was comfort in the deliberate movements because his heart was pounding like a base drum. At the end of the hall, he found her in the bedroom, bra on, tugging up her jeans and buttoning them before she saw him standing there. But she still didn't say anything.

Not a good sign.

"Is something up?" He watched her, noting that her eyes would only focus on him for a moment before she looked back to her task.

"I just need to get home."

Not a no.

He took a deep breath as she shrugged into a t-shirt. She looked too comfortable for the weekend to be heading home with almost no explanation. "Is this because of what I said last night?"

That made her pause... which was probably a yes. *Fuck.*

Riley looked away, her eyes settling on her shoes. Shoving her feet down into them, she hopped for a moment, then stood up straight to look at him, as though she'd needed shoes for whatever she was going to say. "It *is* about that."

She sighed after she said it.

Christian almost stood there like an idiot and blinked at her, but he realized that wouldn't do him any good. So he tried to say something. "You could say you loved me too."

That was dumb. The moment he said it, he knew it was like throwing a bomb into the middle of the room. The air grew thick around him as he worked to suck in oxygen and counted the seconds. He could almost hear a ticking sound in the space between them. When had it gotten so wide?

"So you meant it? It wasn't just something you blurted out?" She was still looking at him almost blankly, still not saying she loved him too.

It was as though she hadn't understood his words. But *I love you* was so simple. So clean. She'd understood, she just didn't want to say it back. Still, he held onto his last shred of hope.

His hands clenched into fists until Christian felt the pressure in his palms. Then he forced himself to let go and relax even if he didn't feel it. "No, I didn't blurt it out."

The space seemed to stretch between them even further. Each rise of his chest was a painful calculation of how much she wasn't saying. Two deep breaths waiting. Three.

"Christian." There was something in her tone that made him pull back. It was the first time he'd not liked hearing his name on her lips. "It's way too early for that."

He didn't know how to answer. What was too early? But this was Riley, she was the one he could talk to, and he did find words. "So, I'm not allowed to feel what I feel?"

"You can't expect me to feel what you feel. Not so fast."

"I didn't." He could feel the heat in his system, anger starting to stir under the surface of his skin. "I never asked you to feel the same way. I just told you how I felt, and now you seem upset about what *I* feel."

"It hasn't been five weeks."

He wouldn't have argued a statement of fact like that, except that her fact was wrong. "It's been nine."

"What?" At least she looked confused rather than hurt and sad.

"We met nine weeks ago, not five."

Her eyes darted to the side as though she didn't want him to catch her gaze. "We started dating five weeks ago, and this is way too fast, Christian. That was out of left field last night."

No, it wasn't. They stayed over at each other's houses three or more nights a week. He almost said so, but when he thought it through, they'd only done that for two weeks. That wasn't long enough to claim it was a habit, but it was certainly long enough for him to feel what he felt.

He didn't know what to say, but Riley did. "I need to go home and just have some time by myself."

She checked around the room, as though to be sure she had everything picked up. Then she made a motion to push past him and he stepped aside before thinking it through. Riley was down the hall, with her jacket on and her purse over her shoulder before he even thought to ask, "Are you coming back?"

🙊 24 🙊

Before he fully understood what had happened, Christian was standing alone in his front entryway, staring at the closed front door. Two half-eaten omelets mocked him, one on the counter as though it had been discarded, and the other still sitting on the table, fully interrupted.

He turned to clean them up, because he needed something to do—something that made sense. He could throw out the eggs, clean the plates and put the kitchen to rights. Washing the plates gave him a clean kitchen. It cleared away the evidence of Riley leaving so suddenly.

He made the bed, straightened the pillows on the couch, and ran the dishwasher. When he had the place looking like she'd never been there, he sat down on the couch and turned on the TV. It took a few moments to choose a show and it was fifteen minutes later that he realized he'd last watched this program almost three weeks ago, before Riley had taken over his life.

When he'd asked if she would come back, she'd said, "I don't know when. I need some time to think."

Christian had no idea what that meant. He'd hoped she'd say Tuesday, or at least Thursday. But Riley had offered him no such solid idea to hold onto. Only "maybe later."

It wasn't enough, but it was all he was going to get.

Going back to the beginning of the program—because he hadn't been paying enough attention to follow—Christian paused it. He wasn't much of a drinker and almost never when he was alone, but today felt like a good time to start.

He rooted through the bottles in the fridge and, when nothing appealed to him, he grabbed the closest thing he thought he might not spit out. Three beers still stared at him— the ones he'd bought for Riley. Christian closed the refrigerator door on the offending bottles and tried not to think about where he'd gone wrong.

Popping the top, he headed back to the couch plopping down with a thud. As he turned the TV show back on he had to wonder, if he loved her, why was that wrong?

Didn't she want him to love her? Wasn't that the whole point of dating?

His mother had always pushed him to find someone. "You'll be happier in a relationship," she'd told him.

"I've tried to get into a decent handful of relationships over the years," he'd protested, "none of them made me happier in the long run."

Those relationships had things wrong with them—things he'd put up with because he wanted to believe his mother was right and if he just rode out the annoyances they would go away. Instead, they'd magnified. He'd broken up with those women, or they with him, and he couldn't say he'd been heartbroken.

Those relationships had gone wrong enough—often enough —that he'd decided to quit trying. His mother was a brilliant woman, and maybe she was right for most people, but not for him. Then Riley had come along. She'd made him think that it wasn't him and it wasn't even the women he'd dated in the past: it was just the wrong match. Raizel Shoshana Zayat was the first one who'd *felt right*.

But obviously, she'd not felt the same about him.

Was he the annoying one? Had he—last night—simply hit a

crescendo of obnoxiousness and Riley couldn't deal with him anymore? Christian honestly didn't know.

His cider was half gone and his show half over when it occurred to him that saying he loved Riley was the breaking point. Were his feelings for her the bad part of their relationship?

That would mean he'd been reading everything wrong all along. That wasn't an impossibility. He'd read things wrong —*very wrong*—before. He just hadn't believed it was like that with Riley. She understood him. So he'd *said* it. Apparently, saying the words out loud was wrong enough to make her head out the door.

Christian had no idea if it was the feelings that were the bad thing or the saying of them. He didn't think about it though, because it didn't matter. Riley was gone either way.

He sat on the couch and stared into space until his phone rang. The TV had cycled through several episodes, none of which he could recall and his drink was empty, though still in his hand when the buzzing brought him around.

Riley.

He didn't have his phone on him and he'd hopped up and run to pick up the phone. "Hello?"

Unable to keep the excitement out of his tone, he plummeted the other direction when his mother answered. "You're bringing deviled eggs tonight, right? Jackson's coming and you know the girls will eat as many as he'll let them."

Christian paused. The normal thing to do would be to go. Make the eggs and show up as if nothing had happened. But that wasn't something he was capable of. They would read him like a newspaper.

"No, mom, not tonight."

"Well, we were counting on you. You can bring Riley."

As if that was any incentive right now. He didn't want to go, and he didn't want to tell her—or anyone—why. "I don't feel well."

It would be one of the very few lies he'd ever told his mother. As a child he'd readily confessed to crimes. As a teenager, he let teachers and other authority figures know when he'd experienced cheating from his work. He'd answer questions as honestly as he could and valued that about himself. But now? He simply couldn't bring himself to say the words.

"—have a temperature? If you didn't take it, you should. Do you have Tylenol? Advil? Those are both good and I'm sure you know what the dosing is." His mother was rambling almost as though she knew it wasn't fully true. "If it's your stomach, heat up some chicken soup, or ramen. You probably have ramen noodles."

"Yes, mom." It was the easier answer. He was certain if he started to talk, he'd spill everything. If she came over now—and she would come over—it would mess up all of dinner for everyone coming. "I'll be okay."

Another lie. He wasn't sure he ever would be okay.

He pulled a second bottle from the fridge. He almost never got drunk. But he now officially had nowhere to be and no one who required him for a few days. If he was waiting out Riley coming back, then he might as well do it drunk.

This time, he left the bottle opener on the counter, almost as an indicator of his plans. Chucking the lid into the trash he watched as he missed and for the first time he didn't care.

Was he nursing a broken heart?

He certainly felt like it, but she hadn't even broken up with him. She'd just said she needed time. Riley hadn't even said what she needed the time for, only that she needed it.

If she was going to come back to him then he needed to man up. That meant stepping back and letting her sort out whatever it was that she needed to be away from him to figure out. But he didn't like it.

The cider was gone before he knew it.

Eventually, he'd finished a full season of the tv show and he wasn't sure he'd seen any of it. He still hadn't figured out exactly what he'd done wrong, only that he must have done it.

His chest felt like it was going to cave in. His brain at last felt fuzzy enough to slow down. Dinnertime had passed and evening had settled in around his house. He didn't have app programming to work on. Christian actually *couldn't* work on it—he needed to cease all further additions until the parent company made a decision that would determine if they kept working with him or if he took his app upgrade somewhere else. Also, he'd had too much to drink to comb over code with any care.

25

Riley watched as Christian carried the paper bag around the room, handing out the appropriate cell phone to each child. It was his last day, despite the fact that it was a Thursday. The Friday class had already finished their projects.

The kids were getting ready to play a game. They didn't understand that it had taken two weeks of work to make it happen. Getting the parents to send the phones and the school to agree to let them into the classroom for this one assignment had been a nightmare. But worth it. Still, this was why Lisa Lynn was the last to present her project.

Christian had shown up yesterday as well, helping with the Wednesday class's last two projects. Patrick still needed a large amount of support from Christian—help Riley couldn't provide. Molly had wanted to show off another program she'd made for the dog. The two presentations had kept both of them busy and they'd hardly talked. Lisa Lynn finally stood at the front of the classroom with Christian just behind her, acting as her on-stage support.

Though he'd barely spoken to her yesterday, today he'd hardly even looked at her. Riley thought maybe that was for the best.

The children, though happy that it was almost the last week before Christmas, had definitely noticed the tension in their teacher. With Christian gone she could get through tomorrow, then just Monday and Tuesday before Winter Break started.

Lisa Lynn pulled herself up to her full—if unimpressive— height, a twinkle in her eye and apple cheeks smiling. She told the class, "Go to the App Store."

It was Christian who put a gentle hand on the child's shoulder and leaned down to whisper in her ear. Lisa Lynn looked up at the group, and asked calmly, "Does everybody have their phone on yet?"

That had to have been Christian's instruction and Riley almost laughed. Turning the device on was one of the biggest hurdles of tech support. She knew at least that much.

She watched as Lisa Lynn carefully waited while the last of the phones booted up then re-issued her first statement. With Christian's guidance, the girl stayed in dynamo mode without breaking down. She walked all the others through downloading the game.

Riley only then realized that Christian must have uploaded it to the app store. It was amazing—Lisa Lynn was only in fifth grade and she had a game in the App Store. Christian had done something truly wonderful for the girl.

Once the kids were going, the next fifteen minutes were spent walking around and checking everyone's download. Several had difficulty getting it installed or started. Riley remembered him having the girl load her game and set it up on as many devices and operating systems as they could find, talking her through all the troubleshooting. He'd even explained that still having trouble was expected. It had worked, because Lisa Lynn stayed calm and collected in the face of several issues.

Once the two were back at the front of the room, looking as though they were surveying their kingdom, Christian leaned over to Lisa Lynn. He pointed at her phone screen. The little girl's breath sucked in on a gasp and she ran immediately to Riley holding the phone up.

"Miss Zayat! A hundred and ten people have already downloaded my game!"

Riley looked at the phone, trying to keep a smile on her face. She'd been excited about the game being in the store, but for the first time she asked the question: did it cost money to get the game? Was Lisa Lynn making money on this? Was Christian?

No, she told herself, it was free for the students to download. And Christian wouldn't make it a paid game in the future. Not without passing the money on to Lisa Lynn's family. So Riley didn't even ask as she looked at the phone screen Lisa Lynn waved at her and smiled wider.

All the little girl had wanted was to make a game that people could play. She'd succeeded and Riley was thrilled for her. Lisa Lynn pushed the phone into her hands, as though Riley had not examined the number thoroughly enough. As she read the description of the game, she felt that old sweet twist in her heart.

Part of the game's beauty was that it was simple—something Lisa Lynn could ultimately almost program by herself. It maintained attention but also didn't play forever and ever. The description included that information but had a subnote with an asterisk: May be helpful for children on the autism spectrum or those with ADHD. Can be an entry game to help focus before starting tasks.

Christian had to have added that, she knew.

"This is great," she said to him, holding up the phone so he could see she was reading the description he'd written for it. Then she handed it to Lisa Lynn, and told the girl, "This is amazing. People are downloading your game already. You did it!"

The little girl was beaming, taking the phone and turning away, watching as the other children in the room played *her* game. Riley was willing to let them tap away on the screens for most of the afternoon. The week had been hard. The usual round of class prep, execution, grading, and following-up had seemed to become a Sisyphean grind the last few days.

A glance across the room told her Christian had pulled up one of the tiny chairs and sat almost in the corner, watching. His long legs came up high enough that he didn't have to lean over to rest his elbows on his knees. One by one, he answered questions as children checked in, but Riley didn't go over to talk to him. She didn't know what to say.

He'd freaked her out on Sunday. She didn't like any of it. They'd been in bed, and she'd screamed his name; he'd moaned hers. Then the words had rushed out of him, *I love you*.

It had been too much. It was still too much, too fast, too much pressure.

It should have been the kind of thing that made her heart soar. As it was, it made her whole body clench. Given that it was said during sex, he very well might not mean it. And what was she supposed to say? So she'd asked, and—being Christian—he *did* mean it.

Even that was a problem. It was possible he was just saving face. Or worse, he *believed* he meant it. Christian had told her he hadn't been in a relationship in quite a while. Neither had she. But she'd been in love before, and she knew better than to just throw those words into the middle of the bed. He hadn't been in love before, so maybe he didn't know, maybe it was all too new to him. But if that was the case, it meant he didn't really know if he loved her or not. Riley was confident he couldn't know at five weeks. Instead of holding back and waiting until he was sure, he'd just gone and blurted it out.

Riley couldn't trust it—that was the problem with those three little words. Worse, it had come on top of other things that had started to make her... uncomfortable wasn't the word, but definitely questioning how they would work these big issues out.

He'd started spending money on her. He'd started catering to her—staying at her place so she could get up in the morning, cooking dinner when she was neck deep in papers. Then he said he loved her.

Listening to her own thoughts, she chided herself. It should have been a dream come true. But she felt as though she would owe him. What happened when he wanted something? Wouldn't she have to bend? Between the money and their schedules, he seemed to suddenly hold all the power between them.

She'd already noticed he wanted something for his life—a partner, maybe a wife—and there was nothing wrong with that, but pushing things forward too fast felt more like a business deal than real love. She'd balked. She still balked at the feeling of it.

Even just sitting here, watching her kids play, her heart ached. Just as it had all week. When Christian showed up yesterday, he'd actually *looked* at her. Before the children appeared from their various classrooms, he'd asked her, "Did you have enough time?"

Jesus. She'd told him she needed time, and he was trying to give it to her. He wasn't angry or combative. He didn't fight or hit below the belt because he was mad. He was sad or hurt or maybe just confused—she couldn't tell—but he was waiting her out. Still, her answer had been "No."

She couldn't trust that he loved her. Not really. Not so fast. And not when he'd been playing along and catering to her. She didn't want to be catered to. She wanted to know what he needed, too. She wanted to be an equal and she wasn't in love with him. Maybe she would have gotten there, but he'd pushed too soon, and she didn't know how to tell him that.

There was no way to ask him to just take it back. That was another problem: When did she want to go back to?

When he was buying her expensive concert tickets, and she was realizing that their monetary situation would never be anything near equal? She would always be on the receiving end of the money. Did she want to go back to the start of things? When they were both nervous and he bought her beer not knowing that she didn't usually drink it either? When she asked him out and he said no, but she hadn't even caught on to why?

She didn't know which part of the relationship had been the good part. Sure, there were wonderful things all along the way, but she'd yet to settle into it. So she scanned the room and watched the clock carefully. She hadn't missed a single class change all week. Riley stood up and called out, "Okay, children. There's five more minutes of play time." But in her brain, she thought *five more minutes to sit with Christian.*

Five more minutes until he leaves for good.

Friday's class was done presenting. He wouldn't be back tomorrow. It was Christian's last day in her classroom. Maybe that was for the best.

When the clock finally hit the top of the hour, she gathered all the cell phones, turning them off and putting them in the bag. Then she told the kids, "Today is Mr. Weaver's last day with us."

Small faces slid into disappointment. Even though they'd been told last week that this would happen, they still looked as though she had just stolen their puppies. One by one, as they left the classroom, each child went up to him. Most of them hugged him and he hugged them back.

"Thank you for my game." Lisa Lynn whispered to him with her arms around his neck. "Will you come back to the classroom and help again?"

Christian had looked up at Riley for the answer, but she hadn't known what to say. Her face had probably remained blank, so he'd looked back at Lisa Lynn not waiting for an official answer. "Probably not. But I'll give you my email and you can reach out to me."

Then he shook his head and looked up at Riley again, this time a question on his face. He clearly was realizing it might not be appropriate to open communication with a fourth grader.

Riley jumped in. "Lisa Lynn, you can tell me what you need and I'll pass it all on to Mr. Weaver." But as she said it, she felt the clenching in her vocal cords. It all felt wrong.

Seven went to high five Christian after Lisa Lynn went out the door, which turned into another hug as well. Riley watched as he interacted with each child, her heart twisting and turning to the point that if she had a heart attack, she wouldn't be able to tell. By the time the room emptied out, she'd figured out what to say.

❦ 26 ❦

Christian looked at Riley. The children were gone and the only thing between them was the air.

"I gathered your things on the shelf over there," she pointed.

So, he thought, she wasn't going to say anything about *them*. Only about the classroom.

She spoke again, maybe just filling the space. He was fine with space. He'd thought she was, too, but not right now, it seemed. "I have bags for everything. You can carry it all easily."

Riley turned then, moving behind her desk, opening a drawer and pulling out colored paper bags with handles. By the time she looked up to see that he hadn't moved from where he stood, she'd tilted her head, but her expression still wasn't welcoming.

"You can keep the things I brought," he told her.

"You can't intend to leave all of this expensive equipment in my classroom." She waved her hand toward the shelf, almost as though it was offensive.

Christian frowned. What had he done wrong? Didn't she want gifts for her classroom? He knew she accepted them from his mother. Hell, she'd asked him into her classroom in the first place because there wasn't enough computer programming and engineering in the curriculum. Fighting down his sigh of frustration, he told her, "I can take it back if you want me to. But my intent was to leave it for the kids. They know how to use it. They have basic programming skills. The motherboards should be great."

When she nodded, he at least felt a little better. At least she didn't tell him that she needed it gone. At least what he had left here wasn't so offensive that she had to get rid of it.

"Okay, then. Thank you. Was that it?" She stood with her hands clasped in front of her, the bags abandoned on her desk behind her, their colors too bright for the stilted conversation.

His face must have flown wide open. He couldn't hide it. Was that the last thing she was going to say to him?

If he turned and walked out the door right now, he might not ever see Riley Zayat again. He almost asked when could they get together? Did she want to go out again? But he feared the answer. Instead, what came out of his mouth was, "Is there ever going to be enough time?"

It didn't really make sense, but Riley understood and at least he didn't have to reframe it and try to say it again.

She'd said she needed time. He'd given her some. Yesterday hadn't been enough. Today, clearly, still wasn't enough. He didn't understand her reaction and he couldn't both give her space and ask her what was going on. He just wanted to know if she was ever going to come back.

"I don't know." She almost whispered it.

Christian felt his heart crack and fall apart right then. He'd been holding it together with hope, but in that moment it all disappeared. He wanted to ask, "What did I do wrong?" But, in truth, he didn't want to know.

It was bad enough that he'd ruined the best thing he ever had, having it labeled and time stamped wasn't going to help. Sure, it could keep him from screwing up the next relationship, but there wasn't going to be a next relationship. He wasn't doing this again.

He wasn't going to fix things. He was just going to go home

and get over it.

"Well," he said, heading for the door for the last time, "Merry Christmas."

He knew he said the right thing. He knew what her family celebrated and he heard her as he was heading out. "Merry Christmas to you too, Christian."

He pulled the door closed behind them. Then headed down to the front of the school, handing in his badge for the last time and getting his driver's license back. The woman at the front desk, whose name it turned out was Karen, asked, "Was this your last day?"

He nodded. Christian knew he should have said something, but it was hard to make his mouth work with his chest in pieces.

"Well, thank you very, very much for being a volunteer at Brighton. And Merry Christmas."

He wished her Merry Christmas in return, but it didn't hurt when she'd said it. Not the way it had hurt when Riley did.

On his last trip to the front door, he saw Riley's friend Angelia coming down the hall.

"Hey, Christian." She waved to him, her smile indicating that she didn't know that he and Riley had broken up. Because apparently they had. He was no longer waiting to hear what the verdict was, it was over. He'd just found out that he had been dumped.

Christian forced himself to find his voice one more time. "Happy Hanukkah."

Her grin widened, glad that he had remembered. He always remembered. It was important to people to get those kinds of things right when you could.

"Happy Hanukkah and Merry Christmas to you," she replied, making him think maybe he should celebrate both holidays. Maybe he should celebrate none of it.

As he pushed the door open into the bitter air, a light rain hit him, making him think that the weather understood his mood. He climbed into the car, his heart cracking as he drove home.

❧ 27 ❧

Compliments should be handed out generously and taken graciously.

RILEY LOOKED OVER THE ITEMS SHE HAD LINED UP ALONG HER couch.

Two of Christian's t-shirts he'd left behind. A toothbrush he had used when he was here. Three of the hard ciders he had brought over. She also liked them, but he paid for them and she thought that made them "his." A bottle of the conditioner his sister had talked him into getting. Apparently, he'd gotten two bottles—one for his place and one for hers. She shouldn't have had an emotional reaction to conditioner, but she did.

Riley looked once down the lineup, then again around her apartment. Her next question was: box or bag?

She did have a cardboard box that everything could pile into. Though it might be spilling out the top. Not very good if she had to leave it on his doorstep. Having it look like a break-up box wasn't very kind. A paper bag with handles might be a little nicer.

Taking a step back, Riley laughed at herself. Maybe Bailey

Ann was right, and she was a Southern Belle. Here she was, contemplating what kind of container to put her ex lover's left-behind items into.

Folding everything she could, Riley set it into the bottom of the bag and stuffed in the rest. She got her butt behind the steering wheel of her car before she could make a different decision and headed toward Christian's house.

Though she considered them broken up, she found she had a spark of hope in her heart. Maybe, if she could explain how she had freaked out and why, they could find some kind of common ground and start over.

In the past, when she'd gone on a mission, she'd had something in mind. She'd always been prepared with some way the problem could be corrected—an apology or paying her back for the rent she'd spent on him or something. Thinking back, Riley couldn't recall a single time she'd actually gotten the thing she needed to fix the problem. Each time had ended in a finality of the breakup.

Still, she remained hopeful, even though she didn't have an item on her checklist. She just had to believe that she and Christian could figure it out.

She was at his door before she thought twice about it, which was probably a good thing. Telling herself she would knock and, if he wasn't home, she would leave the bag on the back porch, she raised her hand.

It took approximately zero seconds once the sound rang out for the door to open and Christian to appear in front of her. She could see the hope in his eyes, too. Maybe they would be okay.

Even though he'd opened the door, he didn't say hello. Just stood there and stared at her. As was often the case, Riley found herself filling in the space. She held up the bag as though to demonstrate she had a purpose.

"I found these things at my place. They're yours, and I thought you might want them back."

He nodded, his hand coming out for the bag. Still zero words spoken from Christian, but Riley didn't hand it over. "Can I come in for a minute? I was hoping we could talk."

Quickly he stepped back. At least he wasn't balking at her idea of having a conversation. Another spark of hope lit in her chest as she took a few bold steps forward. When she was inside and he had closed the door behind her, he finally spoke.

"What did you want to talk about?"

That was something she should have been prepared for: a blunt statement. No easing into the conversation, not with Christian.

Riley swallowed. She could handle a classroom full of seven-year-olds. She could do this. It was probably best to open with an apology. And she owed one to him. "I'm sorry I freaked out."

"So, is that it? It was enough time and you figured it out?" he asked. But she could hear the undertone—he didn't quite believe it. He was right not to.

"No," she said. "I don't have it figured out. I don't know how we fix it. I just know that we were getting off balance before..." she couldn't quite mention the moment that everything had gone to hell. "And—"

"What do you mean we were off balance?" he interrupted.

Shit, she thought, *he hadn't even seen that things had slowly been going a little wrong before he said that.* "You spending that money on concert tickets and dinners. Money that I can't put into this relationship. I can't match it. You don't even work." Well, that was wrong. "I mean, you *do*. I know that. But you work these odd hours and I have a full-time job. Our whole schedule revolves around me and it feels like..." she didn't know what to say and she'd been rambling anyway. She just let it trail off.

He frowned at her. "Our schedule didn't revolve around you. There were plenty of times you came over when I was working—"

"Just that one week." She shouldn't have jumped in.

He frowned again, and Riley didn't like the look of it. This was not the way she had hoped the conversation would go.

"No." He was shaking his head as though she had said the sky was yellow. "You came over late plenty of times. Because I had work to finish. When you went to work, I went to work, too. I clocked eighty-hour weeks most of the time we were together."

Riley tried to stop her jaw from falling open. She'd thought he was living a leisure life. Enjoying the proceeds from his previous program sales. He'd been working *eighty hours a week?* More than her this whole time... and he had hidden it from her so well. "I didn't know."

"Obviously." Though he didn't say it, she could hear the accusation hanging in the air. *You didn't ask.*

Surprisingly, Christian jumped into the void. "That may have been a problem. But you freaked out when I told you that I love you. And that was not the reaction I wanted."

"It's too early," she protested. Riley could feel the emotion rising as the words came out of her mouth without much guidance from her head. She was struggling to rein them back in, but her mouth kept going. "It was a lot of pressure, you saying you love me."

"How is me telling you how I feel pressure on you? I specifically said I didn't expect anything back. It just wanted you to know how I feel."

"But that's just it!" she burst out, "I don't know that! I don't know that's really how you feel. It's way too early!" She was breathing as though she'd been running, the conversation taking its toll. This was not the reconciliation she'd hoped for. "You said you hadn't had a lot of relationships. Maybe you're misinterpreting it. What will I do in two months when you come back and realize that you didn't understand what you were feeling? That you didn't know what it is to really be in love?"

This time it was Christian's mouth that dropped open. When she looked up, Riley saw the damage she'd done, the hurt in his eyes.

Usually she loved that he was an open book to her, but right now she hated it. That was always Christian, raw and real. She'd hurt him and he didn't seem to have the ability to hide that from her.

He, however, managed to operate from his head while her broken heart was taking over everything. Watching as he took several deep breaths, she felt as well as heard the words when he eventually said, "Thank you for bringing my things over. But I think maybe it's time for you to leave."

❧ 28 ❧

Christian hugged his mother goodbye. He fervently hoped that was the end of Christmas Eve for him. He tried to slip out the door and go home to be by himself. But now as she hugged him, she whispered in his ear, "We'll do something for your birthday tomorrow."

"No, mom," he almost begged it. "Please don't."

His chest felt hollow and heavy at the same time, just as it had all week. He was learning to live with it, but it wasn't getting better. Still, he didn't want the half-assed birthday celebration that his family always managed to come up with.

Even regular presents at Christmas time had always seemed overblown to him. Carlisle liked kitchen gadgets and fun nursing related items, like syringe pens or a monogrammed stethoscope. Charlie liked tickets to places he'd never been. But his family didn't know what to get Christian. No one else was into computers and technology the way he was. He wanted a specific program to download. He wanted an external dock that transported information without glitching.

None of those were things that his family knew where to buy, or how to judge the quality on. Many were things he just needed to download to his own system, not the kind of thing that was easily given as a gift. And they weren't the kind of things he wanted to wait around for. He could afford to buy them himself, and a lot of times his family couldn't. Carlisle couldn't get him the gaming computer he wanted, and she couldn't even write it off on her taxes. He could. Them getting him presents made little to no sense to him, and he disliked the forced celebration.

"Honey," she said, "It's your birthday. We want to celebrate."

For a moment Christian stopped and wondered if it was *his* birthday, then shouldn't *he* get to choose how to celebrate? He said something akin to that. "I'd like to celebrate by not celebrating."

At least she seemed to take that for what he said. He hugged her a little tighter and this time he managed to slip out the door. Though, as he slid into his car, he realized she hadn't necessarily agreed to it.

At the first Sunday dinner after the breakup, they'd asked about Riley. "Why didn't Riley come this week?" "Where is Riley?" "How is the gifted class going?"

He'd been forced to mumble out, "We broke up."

It was beautiful in its awfulness, like watching a tornado rip everything up. The very week after he'd introduced his first girlfriend at Sunday dinner, he'd had to tell them all it was over. What a flaming piece of shit.

He'd watched his mother wave her hand around the table. Though he didn't understand it, apparently it was an almost magical signal to everyone else not to ask about Riley again. At least that had been a politeness he'd appreciated.

SixCo had emailed him back earlier in the week, letting him know they wanted the app redesigned and they wanted him to do it. They said they voted and they wanted the app, even if he was going to build in a blockchain firewall.

This was exactly what he had figured would happen. Initially, he'd been afraid that all the extra work and the new, tightened deadline would keep him away from Riley. What a laugh. Now, he was grateful for it.

He'd made it this far. Christmas Eve, late at night, he looked out the back window into the yard that didn't have a swing set or a dog or even a nice lawn. If he was a child, he would have been looking out the window waiting for jingle bells or trying desperately to go to sleep so Santa could come. Outside the cold frosted the corners on all his windows, unusual in Georgia. The night could have been magic. Instead, it was just cold and lonely.

His life had gone back to normal the moment that Riley left his apartment. His skills weren't great, but he knew what that had meant. He'd known things had gone from bad to worse when she said she thought there was no way around it.

This week was almost exactly like the weeks before he'd begun volunteering in her classroom. Only now he knew the old "normal" had been awful.

His mother had hugged him at that Sunday dinner where he'd told them the bad news and whispered in his ear then, too. "It will get better. Eventually, the bad feelings will fade," she said, "and you'll be ready to find someone new."

But that was the problem: he didn't want someone new. He didn't want to do this ever again. And she was wrong about the rest of it, too. The feeling hadn't faded.

Tonight, she'd said he looked like he was doing well. But all that had changed was that he'd developed some slightly better coping mechanisms. If anything, the whole debacle felt worse.

So he headed to his office and his keyboard, to the things that always reacted the way they were intended to. If there was an error, it was *his*. He could comb through the code and find it and fix it. Not like life. Not like Riley.

Shutting out all his other thoughts—Riley, his birthday, Christmas—he opened up the batch of code he was working on and started de-bugging it. It was tedious work, but he was good at it.

This was apparently where he belonged.

❦ 29 ❦

"Mom," Riley said, sitting on the couch next to her mother. "I don't know. I don't know how to fix it."

She loved having her mother here, someone to talk to and bounce ideas off. Someone who knew exactly who she was. Her parents had come in for the Christmas holidays, staying with her grandparents in the spare room, rather than taking up space at Riley's condo. Maybe next time, Riley would go home and see her old friends but, for now, it was nice to have her mother come to her. Her grandmother was hosting all the events and Christmas Eve dinner was over. She and her mother had finally been left alone.

Her mother, of course, had immediately asked about Christian. Shocking Riley, her mother didn't ask her to explain. Instead she said, "Tell me about him."

Initially, Riley thought of the easy things. He was tall, with chestnut brown hair, green eyes, and an easy smile. Or he had an easy smile once he got to know you. His moss green eyes showed everything he was feeling... once he decided to let someone in.

Still, that wasn't what she told her mother. What she said out loud was, "He's crazy smart, *so* smart. He skipped grade levels, but nobody ever helped him catch up when he didn't fit in socially. He's crazy generous. He's made a bunch of money on his apps. But it's not just the donations of all the equipment to the classroom, it's his time. He came in three times a week, when he was working eighty-hour weeks already on his own projects, and he never missed a day. He learned all the children's names the first week and he knew what they each liked to do. So even if they didn't like coding or running the robots with him, he knew what to say to them."

"And what was he like with you?" her mother asked, making Riley realize that even though she wasn't discussing what he looked like, or the soft thermal shirts that he favored, she'd still been holding him at bay.

"He got me concert tickets, and he worked around my schedule to the point that I didn't even realize he was working as much as he was. He cooked me dinner when I was working too hard. I mean, I cooked him dinner, too. That went both ways," she corrected, realizing she'd started babbling again.

Her mother stayed sitting calmly, acting like the attorney that she was. She waited until she caught Riley's gaze and didn't allow her to look away. Her mother's face mirrored Riley's own, dark hair framing her eyes and her serious expression.

"He sounds like a dream. So, why did you leave?"

"Because we were lopsided, Mom. He had all the money, and what do I bring to the situation?" Realizing her mother was going to get everything out of her eventually, Riley decided to just spill everything. "And then he said he loved me, and it was way too soon. I don't trust that he actually loved me. I'm afraid —" there it was, the moment of truth her mother had been digging for. "I'm afraid he'll figure out in a few months that it wasn't real. And that he didn't know because he hasn't been here before."

Just like when she was speaking to Christian earlier, her mouth had run on without her. But she'd finally run dry.

Her mother nodded. "That makes sense. But what is it that makes you not trust him?"

Suddenly, Riley faltered. There was no answer to that. Why didn't she trust him?

Now, at home in her own condo, she had been thinking about that more and more. Westerley Weaver's words came back to her ears. "I had a template for how everything should go, and everything went according to plan until Christian came along. That boy never did anything on my—or anyone else's —timeframe."

He hadn't done anything on Riley's either and that was the problem.

She had a timeframe and a plan. She knew how long they should date before they said they loved each other. How long after that before they should move in.

Christian didn't. Christian moved at his own pace.

As far as trusting what he said, Riley had to stop and rethink that too.

There is no reason not to trust him.

The fact was, it was one of the things that she loved about him. He was always honest. He never pulled punches. He said "probably" instead of "yes" if he wasn't sure. She'd loved that when he said she was beautiful, she believed him. Riley wasn't necessarily certain that she was beautiful, but she believed that was what he saw.

There was no player in him. No game. No trying to get ahead. If he said he loved her, he'd done it just for the sheer purpose of telling her how he felt.

While she was scared that how he felt wasn't real, there was absolutely no reason to believe that she was right. In fact, she was *wrong*.

All this time, she'd been sitting here thinking that this was Christian's issue. That he'd pushed too hard, too fast. That he hadn't seen they were off balance. He had been paying for too much. But as he said, she provided a lot to the relationship, too —something he hadn't found anywhere else. She just hadn't valued what she provided.

She'd overvalued the money. He hadn't.

It was an easy thing for him to give. So he'd given it to her and she'd been afraid he'd expect a quid pro quo of some kind. But that wasn't Christian. That was just her own fear and bias talking.

Her heart was beating faster as her mother's questions and her own answers churned in her head. Westerley Weaver had been right about her son. It was Riley who'd been too rigid, too fenced in by her own expectations to see what was in front of her.

She considered getting in her car and running to him to apologize right now. See if he would take her back. Tell him she loved him, too.

It was supposed to get easier over time if you broke up with someone. But that seemed to be true only with someone you were *supposed* to break up with. She'd even been in love before. When she'd left, it had felt better. Freer. Like a new chapter.

Breaking up with Christian only felt worse. She wasn't freer, she was caged. She didn't have a new chapter, only a bleaker future without him. All those things felt worse every day than the day before.

Because she missed him with all her heart. Because she needed to stop worrying about the things that she was afraid of and start paying attention to the things Christian actually said.

Riley had her keys in her hand, and her cell phone in her pocket before she thought better of it. Instead—with a better idea, one that Christian deserved—she hopped on her computer. Shooting off a handful of emails to the parents of her students, she crossed her fingers and hoped they could spare a little time on Christmas.

Then she hit the kitchen and began baking.

🙊 30 🙊

Christian was considering taking a nap. It was only two in the afternoon, but his mother had fed him so much food that there was no way he could think through getting any work completed.

He'd woken up early, showered, dressed, and headed over to have Christmas with his family. Charlie had sent him a piece of local art from one of the places that he photographed. That, Christian thought, was a useless but *fascinating* trinket. And he loved it.

Carlisle had bought him a fitness watch. Though he'd originally thought it was beneath him, she pointed out that the one she got was baseline and fully programmable. She added that it would now substitute for his alarm clock, cell phone, and more. All depending on what he did with it. It was pretty ingenious that she'd managed to get him his programs, without having to do it herself.

His mother had gotten him the blanket.

"It's weighted!" she'd declared with glee. "Try it!" And she'd gone on to practically force him to open the box and take the gift out. So he'd sat on the couch, like a child with his blankie for the remainder of the morning. He had to admit it did feel good, but it had been a little hard to fold it all up properly and get it back into the box.

Now, he stood in his office, looking at the walls and wondering where he might hang the art Charlie had sent him. Unable to decide, he left it propped on the desk and headed into his bedroom where he set the box with the blanket on his bed, before wandering back out to the living room.

He was setting up his new fitness watch, when the knock came on the door. Assuming he'd forgotten something at his parents' house, and that either they or Carlisle were dropping it off, he merely pulled the door open. Christian was shocked to find Riley standing there, uncertain what to say. He pulled out the only thing he could.

"Merry Christmas."

But she shook her head. "Nope. No Christmas here. It's your birthday."

He saw then that she had a wrapped package tucked under one arm. Next he noticed that it wasn't Christmas paper, but a print of colored balloons beneath the bright blue bow, a tag hanging off, twisting in the light wind. A large bag hung from her other hand.

"May I come in? I come bearing birthday gifts."

His heart stuttered in his chest. And he didn't want it to. He didn't want to give in to the hope that flared with her visit. *She'd remembered his birthday.*

The best birthday present would be getting Riley back. If that wasn't happening, he wasn't sure what good the rest of this would be. Still, he stepped back and waved her in. She had come bearing gifts, after all.

Sweeping past him—she knew his home almost as well as her own—she headed to the table. That silly table he'd bought for their first date. It still had the same tablecloth on it, though certainly he'd washed it several times in between.

Setting the gift box down, Riley carefully laid the bag onto one of the chairs. She pulled out a bottle of champagne, then opened a cardboard box he'd not seen was inside. From the box, she pulled out a mid-sized cake.

Leaning over, he read the top.

Happy Birthday, Christian.

Everything in him felt like the clench in his jaw when he ate too much sugar too fast. He didn't know what to do. He hoped he could just wait it out and—like the sugar problem—it would resolve itself in just a moment. But it didn't.

Riley turned to look at him. "Happy birthday. I have several presents."

"You brought me a cake." It was a dumb thing to say, but it tumbled out of his mouth. The whole situation seemed surreal and generated far more hope than was reasonable.

Riley shook her head. "I *made* you a cake. I make good cake."

He smiled and said, "I've never had any cake that you've made before."

"That's fine," she replied. "You can be the judge of it, but it's good cake. I'm realizing there are things that I do that are valuable between us. Maybe making cake is one of them."

That didn't make much sense to him, but he wasn't about to ask and burst the bubble he was in. It was surreal—this conversation felt as though they were together, or at least friends, but not that they hadn't been speaking for several weeks. "Can I cut it and take a slice?"

"Not yet," she said. "First, I got you this." She pulled up her phone and tapped a few buttons, making him curious what it was. But, just as he was getting impatient, she said, "Okay, it's in your email now."

He tapped at his watch, but the email feature hadn't installed yet. So he headed across the room, picked up his phone and opened what she had sent. It took a few minutes to watch it all the way through. A video had bloomed on his screen, put together from a simple online program probably, but it contained birthday wishes from most of the kids he'd had in her classes.

His heart started to melt a little, even though he shouldn't let it. It melted even as he reminded himself that he'd told her he loved her and she'd left. But he couldn't stop feeling it. He was going to be vulnerable to whatever she said to him today. He knew that. Christian braced himself.

"You told them it was my birthday."

"Yes," she replied, "I emailed the families. Please don't hold it against the kids who didn't respond, they may not have gotten it yet."

"And you put it all into the video." He knew because the last one had said, "Happy birthday, love, Riley." Did it say *love* Riley, because that was the normal way to sign a message or did she *mean* it?

Christian wished he didn't care so much. But it was yet another thing that he couldn't stop.

"Another gift." She said, thrusting forward the brightly wrapped box, and breaking through the tide of his feelings.

He had to take it from her. She was holding it out almost into his face. When he opened it, he saw several t-shirts. That, at least, brought him down a notch or two. She'd gotten him t-shirts. But she seemed to understand the expression on his face, and Riley shook her head.

"Those aren't just any shirts. They're made from bamboo. The seams are all flat. There's no tag. And they're just a little bit thicker than normal, so they're super soft." She smiled, then commanded, "Touch them."

Placing his hand uncertainly into the box, Christian softly petted the top shirt. His breath sucked in; she was right. They felt like heaven. Maybe she'd gotten him t-shirts, but she'd been paying attention.

Jesus what was he going to do when she said *Happy Birthday*, and left?

As he looked up he saw she was pulling out candles and putting several on the cake.

"I don't need candles," he protested. He wanted to say, *I don't need you*. But it wasn't true.

"But I need something to do," she replied, pushing the last candle into place. Riley lit the candles and turned around and said, "I'm sorry I didn't believe you. And... I love you."

With her hands clasped in front of her, she waited for him to reply.

༄ 31 ༄

Christian felt his heart jump into his throat. Those words made him want to take her in his arms, kiss her, take her to bed, eat the cake. But none of those things were really an option. They'd barely spoken to each other for two weeks.

So he forced himself to ask the hard questions. "Why do you love me now, when you didn't love me when I said it?"

Riley looked away. Only this time, she wasn't so much avoiding him as she looked ashamed. That bothered him, but he waited until she spoke. "I did love you. I just hadn't figured it out yet, and I was freaked out by you saying it so soon."

She paused and Christian waited. "I had a timeframe. Everyone knows how long you date before you say you love someone. How long to wait before it's okay to move in together. How long before you get engaged. Or get married."

He could feel his brows pulling together, his mouth curling up.

She saw it, too. "Exactly. Everyone knows this, except you."

"Thanks," he replied wryly. Still, she wasn't wrong. But maybe she didn't have to come over and point it out.

"No. That's just it, Christian. I got on your case for breaking rules. But you didn't break any rules. You didn't know they were rules. You were just on your own time frame. *And I wasn't.* I was on a time frame that wasn't even created for me, and I let it dictate what I do. I shouldn't have."

Slowly, the little candles burned down, leaving wax on the pretty cake while she talked. But he let her have her say; she seemed to have more of it.

"You scared me, Christian." When he started to protest, Riley held up her hand to hold him off. "That isn't on you. That's on me. All this time, I thought you were the one going off track. And the thing was, you were on track. You were just on your own track, and I was the one trying to put you on a different one. It was so soon. I just didn't believe you could actually feel those things for me. The way you spent money on me, it felt like you had gone overboard. But the fact is, you've never lied to me. I remember thinking that I loved that you were always so honest and that I trusted you when you said things. But the thing is, when you got mad at me about that last week, when I came over, you were right."

She paused and this time she looked at him. "Because it isn't trust when it's easy and obvious. It's really only trust when it's hard. It's trust when there's no evidence behind it. If I trust you, then I have to trust what you said. And I'm going to trust that you actually love me. I'm going to trust that you buy expensive things because you have the money and that you aren't looking for anything in exchange. I'm going to trust—and please remember, this is hard for me—that I bring things to this relationship as valuable as what you bring."

How had she thought she didn't bring valuable pieces to the relationship? It seemed all he brought was money and there were a million assholes with that. But as he felt his brain and heart tumbling over each other, he realized that what she was waiting for was for him to trust her too.

He felt the pressure building up behind his eyes at the back of his jaw. Tension pulled between his shoulders, and every cell of his body was on fire. But he wanted to believe her.

"What happens the next time I screw up?" he asked.

"I don't know," Riley said. "But I won't leave. I won't tell you to leave. And I won't bail. I'd ask about the next time I screw up, but you already proved yourself. I figure we'll have to establish some kind of ground rules. We have to figure out if we can call time-outs or whether we're willing to fight in public."

Christian shook his head *no* to that one. Fighting in public was a hard *no*, but Riley was nodding at him that rule was okay, and a small smile started to form on her lips. "Those kinds of things."

Christian jumped in. "We haven't defined how much money we can spend on concert tickets, Riley, and that seems to be important. How many times can I buy dinner? How much can it cost? We don't have anything defined! How can this be okay?"

"There will always be surprises," she said. "There will always be new things and we'll have to work them out. The question is whether or not we want to work them out together. I'm willing to figure all of that out with you. No, I'm not just willing, I *want* to."

"I did want to figure it all out with you," he protested, the sensation boiling up out of him. "And you disappeared."

"I know. I'm so sorry, and I can tell you that I won't do it again. If I screwed up too badly, and you can't trust me anymore, I understand." She waved her hand toward the table, gesturing toward the cake. "I hope you have a happy birthday... And, I love you. Whatever you decide, I love you."

❧ 32 ❧

Riley finally stopped talking. She had said everything she needed to say.

Now, all that was left to do was wait to watch the little candles burning down. They'd hit the halfway point, leaving little wax puddles next to them in the frosting.

She'd worked hard on that cake. Baking, slicing, filling it with homemade frosting and then decorating it. Thinking about that was easier than waiting to hear if he would forgive her.

She didn't know but he was looking at her. So she forced herself to look him in the eyes as she waited.

Finally, he spoke. "I didn't stop loving you just because you walked away. I said *I love you* in the first place, not expecting you to love me back—"

"But I do, Christian. I'm sorry it took me so long to figure it out, but I do. And I trust you." Each time she said it. The *I love you* got a little easier.

Each time he spoke, her trust grew more foundation to build on.

He didn't say anything, only took a few steps closer to the table and closer to her. Then he leaned over and blew out the candles.

"Happy birthday," she whispered. "Whatever it is, hope you get your wish."

He was so close she could smell him. He smelled like the conditioner in the bottle she'd brought back to him. He smelled like comfort. And love. And home.

When he stood up. He was so near that all she had to do was lift up on her toes, and she could kiss him. Slowly—so he could back out if he wanted—she did exactly that.

The kiss lasted about half a second in its tentative first touch, but then burst into flames. His arms came around her, holding her tight, before he reached up her back and finally held her head.

Christian's mouth ravaged hers. Riley melted into his touch, and then he whispered a word across her lips.

"Stay."

"Yes," she whispered back, kissing him fiercely, her heart suddenly light enough to float. The air full of helium making her high.

She reached for him, holding him closer—as if that was possible—when he pulled back again. Holding her a few inches away so he could look her in the eyes, he said, "No, don't just stay, stay *forever*."

Riley looked up at him, as the world suddenly came grinding to a halt. The universe stopped turning, and the night sky waited with bated breath. But none of it mattered. Christian's love was exhilarating. It was petrifying that she might one day lose it. It was a foundation to build everything else on top of.

"Yes." She reached for him to kiss him again.

But Christian only smiled. "Got my birthday wish."

Riley laughed as her world started turning again and she kissed this amazing man with everything she was worth.

❧ 33 ❧

M*imosas solve all problems*

BAILEY ANN SETTLED HERSELF AT THE SMALL ROUND TABLE. IT would have seated four, but held only herself and Riley and Angelia. Three placemats held settings for them to eat their dinner. The fourth setting had a partially eaten cake under a glass dome.

"I'm impressed," she told Riley, "You kicked my cousin out of his own house for a ladies night."

"Well, actually," Riley replied, "I told him what I wanted to do and he pretty much ran for the hills."

"But why not your place?" Angelia asked as she set out a beautiful salad at each setting and headed back into the small kitchen where Riley had prepped pasta alfredo.

"Because this is my place now."

Bailey Ann's mouth wanted to fall open, but she didn't let it. Her Mama had trained her too well. Every time she let her mouth fall open as a kid, she was told, *You look like a cow*. But man, did she want to look like a cow right now. She tried to cover by pouring the champagne and juice evenly into the glasses. Still, she asked, "You moved in together? It's not even New Years! Wow."

"I know," Riley sighed the words out, but Bailey Ann knew that sigh. It was a contented one. "Christian said he knew what he wanted and I... didn't."

"I remember," Bailey Ann murmured. She'd gotten an earful when Aunt GiGi and Aunt Westerley had taken her and Carlisle out for a "girl's lunch" last week. As far as she knew, Riley and Christian had still been broken up then, though none of them knew enough to say why.

Riley raised her glass to them. "I figured it out. *I want Christian*. And we decided to try two weeks here and then if we want, we'll try two weeks at my condo and just be sure it's all working. Then we'll decide to stay here or there, or move to a totally new place."

Bailey Ann almost spit out her wine as she laughed. "That sounds exactly like my cousin!"

"He's very scientific about it," Riley conceded, seeming to enjoy her friend's laughter. "But I have a hard time arguing with it."

"Well, if it works for you," Angelia pointed with her glass as she seated herself at the table, "then hang on to it. I'm just bummed that man is off the market."

They ate and talked about Christmas and Angelia's Hanukkah celebration with her family. But Bailey Ann didn't fool them for long.

"What's eating at you?" Angelia looked at her as though she could see right through her friend.

"You won't believe what I did... what I *do*." She watched as Riley and Angelia exchanged a quick glance to each other then laser focused on her. She'd opened this can of worms, and she'd probably done it because she needed someone to talk to. "I guess it's just being back in my hometown and taking care of Daddy and all that, but I walk around the neighborhood. Even in this cold weather..."

That wasn't it. It wasn't about the walks and she wasn't fooling her friends.

"But I walked by Finn Malloy's house yesterday—"

"Finn Malloy?" Angelia almost gasped it, but then she turned and explained it to Riley. "They were hot and heavy in high school. Everyone thought they'd get married but this one—" she pointed to Bailey Ann, "ended it before she went to college. Hearts broke across town over it!" Then she turned back to laser-gaze at Bailey Ann again. "So, you walked by and clearly something happened... tell us before we wring it out of you."

It was silly. She didn't know why she'd brought it up. "It seems like someone is living there again."

Her friends were looking at her, but it was the kick in her heart that scared her. Hope could be a dangerous thing. Especially, when you already knew the two of you didn't work.

AFTERWORD

Did Christian set your soul on fire like he did mine? Maybe this is the first story of mine you've read, but if it isn't then you already know I love *that guy*. The one who might be shy, but has hidden depths. The one who isn't the smooth player but somewhere under there his game is actually spot on. I love that Christian is a little too honest for his own good, but there's a benefit to that honesty: Riley knows that he means exactly what he says! Though I made Christian's test results that he's not on the Autism Spectrum, I think it's clear that he's close. His uniqueness brings so much to this romance, and Riley's lifelong passion of teaching gifted kids allows her to see the man underneath.

If you keep reading the Breathless, Georgia series, you'll get to see his sister Carlisle find her perfect match and younger brother Charlie return home to find he can't shake the things he's seen.

I created the Mayfair/Waverly family so you could fall in love with them as much as I did. I hope you enjoyed the journey to Riley and Christian's happily ever after. If you did and you want to leave a review, it would make my day. Thank you so much!

PREVIEW OF PERFECT
(BREATHLESS, GA - BOOK 1)

There should always be fine liquor on hand, you never know when a gentleman might want some. You never know when you might need some yourself.

"Bailey Ann Mayfair, when are you going to marry me?"

Bailey spun around on the street, looking for the voice that was a pure blast from her past. The sound was both sweet and spun with regret. She peered into a wind that felt far more bitter than it should have, but that was likely just her mood.

He'd asked that same question of her more than once before. He'd asked it in jest and in full sincerity. And now he was asking on the street of Breathless, Georgia, where anyone could hear. But Bailey Ann hadn't seen him in at least five years.

Her eyes searched the street until she landed on him. She didn't recognize him by sight, but she knew just by feel that the broad-shouldered form standing down the street was Finn Malloy. Her face lit up; she could feel it. "Finn! I didn't know you were in town."

She fought the urge to run and throw herself into his arms, to sink there and let him lift away all the world. But she was out in public, so she couldn't do it. She'd also answered that same question in the negative before—a good indicator that he wasn't going to take kindly to her using him as a crying shoulder if she tried it.

He walked closer, the straight nose and bright eyes so familiar. The broad mouth almost smiling, but not quite. Typical black Irish coloring marked him. His hair was so dark as to be inky, his eyes blue enough to be startling. She'd once told herself she couldn't marry a man with prettier eyes than her own.

Even in his twenties, he'd been slim but cut. Something had happened, and he now filled out that suit he was wearing. She blinked. "You're wearing a suit."

"Yeah," his mouth got closer to smiling, but still didn't quite achieve it. "I do that. I wear a suit."

She only nodded, because what else could she say? That she didn't think he'd been the type? That she'd never seen him in one before? Weren't jeans more his style? It all sounded vaguely insulting and she'd been carefully taught to never insult someone unless she meant it. Tears pushed at the back of her eyes, and Bailey fought them back. "Are you doing something specific here?"

Breathless wasn't the kind of place a person visited without a purpose. It was full of families and homes and schools. The shops were cute, the diner was full-scale Southern with a capital S, and the main street was named "Main" and lined with the basic stores with pretty lettering, but it wasn't a tourist town.

"I'm taking care of my parents' house," he finally answered her, the words not quite sinking in.

"Oh, did they move out? Somewhere flatter?" She was thinking of old knees and all the stairs in the house. It was a kind way of asking if they'd been moved to a nursing home, or more, when she noticed he was looking at her oddly.

"No. The house is all that's left. They died in a car accident about a year ago."

"What?" She stopped cold. "They . . ." She couldn't bring herself to say it. She'd had no idea. How had she had no idea?

Finn nodded solemnly. "Single car. They went into the big tree over on Kellar, but neither of them made it."

"Oh, my God, Finn, I'm so sorry." Truly, she was. But she was just as sorry that she hadn't known. That she hadn't come back and attended their funerals. Mrs. Malloy had no more approved of Bailey being her son's girlfriend than Bailey's own mother had approved of "that immigrant boy." Still, it didn't seem right to not attend. It was worse to not have known.

He just nodded. "After your mother passed, I figured you probably weren't getting the news." He shoved his hands in his pockets, the conversation awfully awkward for two people who'd had some of the most amazing sex she'd known existed. For someone who'd asked her to marry him on multiple occasions.

This time, he was the better person and bridged the silence for them. "When is the service for your father?"

Just being asked, just having to think about it again pushed the tears forward. "Saturday morning at the church." She took a beat before she realized she wasn't being clear. "Our church, First Methodist on South Main. We'll have a reception at the house afterward."

He nodded again. Though she hadn't gotten the news about an accident with both his parents, and though she had family and friends in town at the time, somehow Finn—with no family left around town—had heard about her father passing within just a few days.

She stepped in. "Are you planning to attend?"

It was all so formal and stilted, she thought. This was Finn. Finn Malloy who'd sat behind her in seventh grade English class. Mayfair. Malloy. They'd been placed next to each other that whole year and the next, too. Finn Malloy, the boy she'd accepted a shy request for a date from. Finn who she'd lost her virginity to before heading off to college. Bailey Ann pushed her hands down into her pockets.

"Am I invited?"

It was a silly question and he probably knew that. Of course, he was invited. The whole town was. Breathless wasn't that big. People who'd known Con Mayfair would simply show up at the church and many, if not most, would follow Bailey Ann and her sisters back to the house. "Of course, you're invited, Finn."

"He didn't like me all that much."

"He didn't like anyone I dated," she retorted quickly to put Finn at ease, but realized quickly that her offhand remark bore a disturbing resemblance to the truth. She covered it with a smile and a straighter spine.

Finn graciously changed the topic. "Are your sisters coming in?"

"I don't know if you heard, but Harper Rose lost her husband about six months back." She didn't add that it was a big fat mess and her little sister had slowly been learning that her husband had no money, they didn't own the house, and he appeared to have no real job. "She's got three little girls to bring with her."

Harper Rose followed in the family footsteps but had her kids much closer together than their parents had. Bailey Ann had yet to find the man to make her a wife. So here she was at thirty-four, talking to Finn Malloy who was gracious enough not to ask if she was still single. She was so boringly single that she'd quit her job and dropped everything to come home when her Daddy called her. She didn't want to dwell on that. "Emma Kate should be in soon, too, but she's working on getting her classes squared away."

At least, Bailey Ann hoped she was. Somehow, she was now the de facto head of this little family of sisters.

"Well, I'm here if you need me." He had his hands still in his pockets but gestured with the flaps of his coat. "It was good to see you, Bailey Ann. It always is."

With that, he turned and walked down the street away from her as she watched. From behind, the wool coat covered the suit that had been a surprise. She saw now that he had on polished shoes and his haircut had been far more expensive than the ones he'd had in school. When she'd known him, he'd been a jeans and t-shirt kind of guy.

When they'd dated, he'd been creative—picnics, hikes, drives out of town. Only rarely did he take her to the movies and even less often to dinner. In the beginning, she'd thought it was just Finn. When he wore the same pair of slacks the second time they'd gone out somewhere nice, she'd started to get a clue. Later, when she'd been in his house, she'd understood.

The Malloys didn't have the extra money for those things. They weren't poor per se, but it seemed they'd spent all their money on the house on Sparrow Road. Their son was in a good neighborhood of a small town, and he was getting a good education at the public school, but they weren't eating steak every week. They weren't getting the threadbare carpets replaced or the front door painted. And Finn wasn't giving her the impression that one day he'd wear wingtips with his perfectly cut suit and fine wool coat.

Then again, he'd always been a surprise.

Bailey found her first smile that day and headed further down the street away from Finn. Toward the corner pizza shop to get a slice and a coke. She needed it. The bad-for-you lunch would provide three of the four food groups—salt, sugar, and grease. She could get the fourth—alcohol—when she got home. She'd decided she was going to open the decanter to Daddy's whiskey and take her first drink of it.

Not that she hadn't had whiskey before, but Daddy had never let her drink in front of him, and he'd never let her have even a sip of the stash he kept at the house. Today, she might need the whole bottle. She had a funeral to plan and a man to get off her mind.

Thank you for reading! I love romances with real love and believable characters, and I hope you found all that in these pages. I want to fall in love right along with the characters, and I do, while I'm writing it.

About Savannah

I started writing when I was eight—I hand wrote an 80-page novella that I believed to be (adult) romantic suspense. I'm proud to say, I've gotten a lot better since then. I've grown up to be a nerd at heart! I love neuroscience and people watching, and if you look, you'll find some of that in each Savannah Kade book. Most days you'll find me in my office, looking out my window at a handful of the neighbor's cows, or watching my dogs or my cat roam the backyard.

Follow me, find me, ask me questions! I would love to hear from you.
www.SavannahKade.com
Savannah@SavannahKade.com